The Red Dress

and Other Stories

Praise for *The Red Dress and Other Stories*

"*The Red Dress and Other Stories* is an array of short stories that holds the tenderness of humanity in a world of chaos. It is loaded with glimpses of dreams amongst the madness, in different countries, about relationships, breakups, get togethers, the honouring of cultural differences and, in particular, women holding each other. The personal adventures of each character are adapted into narratives where love and kindness seep in to heal a hurting history."

—MARGARET KAYE

"In *The Red Dress and Other Stories*, Heidi Harrison captures the moments that alter the course of a life—sometimes quietly, sometimes with startling force. Each story unfolds at the crossroads of choice and consequence, where ordinary people confront the extraordinary within themselves. Through her lucid prose and keen emotional insight, Harrison reveals how change often comes uninvited, yet leaves behind unexpected strength and grace. From fleeting encounters to lifelong reckonings, these stories explore what it means to grow, to break, and to begin again. Poignant and deeply human, *The Red Dress and Other Stories* is a testament to transformation—a reminder that even the smallest shifts can reshape a life entirely."

—MANDA BURGESS

"This is a remarkable collection of stories—noteworthy for the breadth, depth, and range of topics, settings, and characters. Written with both clarity and vividness, Ms. Harrison's voice shines forth through multi-layered characters who struggle, triumph, and speak a unique truth about being human and living in a complex world."

—DIANE CHIRA

"In her first story, The Red Dress, the sacred red is juxtaposed with sophisticated, ornate rubies revering hope and survival, where the outpouring of emotions is coloured with each violin note taking us to unknown places or long forgotten. Heidi expresses in her writing loss, despair and grief with compassion, beauty, and a raw passion. In all her stories, Heidi expresses very beautifully the importance of tribal roots, the bond among women, and the everlasting healing that emerges when we honour our lineage and ourselves as women. It is then when real freedom can flourish in all its magnitude, a sense of being truly alive."

—JEY IBARRA

Other books by Heidi Harrison

The Four Seasons

When Paris Was Her Lover

Quand Paris Était Son Amour

From the Outside

The Red Dress

and Other Stories

Heidi Harrison

EMERALD HOUSE PUBLISHING

www.emhoup.com

Printed in the United States of America
First Edition—January 2026

Cover Design by Sharon Blyth-Moss
Book Design by Gorham Printing

To my mother who is my everything and to my Baba because finally, now in her home, I sleep peacefully.

TABLE OF CONTENTS

THE RED DRESS

There was a red dress. It was a ruby of a dress, bigger than life, bejeweled by a story that has not been told yet. And somewhere in the folds of memory, this story and this dress needed a voice.

The dress was found in an old chest that had been buried under the earth. This is a story about obscurity: sometimes the best discoveries were hidden at first.

Occasionally, though, History alters this.

* * *

For a month, they had been hiding in dusty closets in their one-hundred-year-old farmhouse in Katowice, Poland, knowing the inevitable would happen. Indeed, that moment came.

In the middle of the night, there was a pounding on the door–harsh German voices. The men forced themselves into the house. Without even the time to make sure the yellow stars of David were securely fashioned onto their coats, Lucia, her two younger sisters, her mother and her father were ripped away from their lives to the ominous world outside their front door. In the darkness, they were shoved first into trucks, and then onto trains crammed with masses of bodies screaming out for God's help, in a time where God was nowhere to be found.

Their final stop was Auschwitz, a soulless ghost destroying all of humanity.

Upon their arrival, guards forced each person to make two lines. Lucia's two sisters and her mother, who had all inherited the gene for smallness and fragility were pushed in the first line. Lucia and her father, robust in size and shape, were put in the second. Everyone in the first line would be gassed within a few hours.

* * *

Lucia clutched onto her father's hand and felt her own strength dissolve into it. For several years at school, she had been called "The Ox", mercilessly ridiculed for her unfeminine body and muscled physique. At seventeen, there was little she could not do. Ironically, this strength now meant survival and gave her a future in a time of life where being the chosen one was all that mattered.

She turned off all emotions the moment she watched her beloved family march into their own graves. Her head spun in a million directions as vomit collected in her throat.

The guards visually inspected her up and down, laughing at her masculine figure.

"Ah! Make this girl dig. Won't take away her cunt that we can use too!" They all laughed together.

Lucia, knowing German, wanted to spit at each of them and tear apart their cocks, making them limp and useless for life. She forced herself to pretend that she did not understand a word they were saying.

They marched on, unaware of the thoughts going through her head.

The next day, she realized she would not be allowed to see her father. That first day when his hand squeezed hers, she saw that the men whispered something to each other. From then on, she noticed that they made sure the two would be far away from each other.

Lucia felt utterly alone in her quest to survive. She thought often of her father. She adored him, a man who combined a sensitivity to the world with an ability to endure. Her inner strength was derived from the love she had for her father, the only surviving member of her family.

Given only a shovel, she was commanded to dig—sixty hours a week. Fortunately, she knew how. She had lived on a farm for her entire life, and shovels had become an extension of herself. What the guards did not know—and what she did not dare tell them—was that they had given her an "easy" job. She feigned ignorance around them and pretended that she had never held a single tool, so that they would see how quickly she could learn and thus leave her alone.

Her ploy worked. They paid little attention to her.

Camp officials had been given orders to install a new state-of-the-art plumbing system for the opulent families of the elite officers. Lucia, however, had no idea why she was digging. While she dug, her mind roamed, and moved freely through a space where she was not a prisoner, where, in the act of moving dirt and forging holes in the earth, she could escape. The soil had always been a comfort to her, soft and pliable, warm and smelling of life.

Ten hours a day she dug, six days a week. At the end of the day, her muscles were sorer than they had ever been. Her body ached with fatigue that obliterated her mind, making it numb, making all things a blur in the conscious self. She did not keep track of time, day, or season.

There were a dozen or so other prisoners around her doing the same work. Except during the occasional rest time they were given, she kept to herself, communing with the earth in silence. Their digging forged deep tunnels into the bowels of some building that Lucia could not see but sensed.

One day, as she was digging a few meters apart from the others, her shovel slammed into something that was not dirt. A sliver of wood came out. She did not dare dig in that area again and figured out a way to work around it, so that the other prisoners would not only not go there but also would not see that she was up to something. When the whistle blew, hours later, signaling that it was time to stop digging for the day, Lucia felt a lightness in her chest, as she maneuvered her way out of the tunnels, past the guards, and through her evening, maintaining her usual painful, yet indifferent expression. She had learned quickly how to look so that the guards would think that she was doing and experiencing exactly what they wanted of her.

At night on her cot, she would usually collapse from exhaustion, and her body, overcome by the strenuous efforts of the day, would quickly succumb to sleep.

That night, though, she feigned to sleep as she carefully watched the guard on duty. He was an older man, and around midnight, he would fall asleep until around 3am, at which point he would wake up and resume his watch. Lucia observed this behavior for three consecutive nights, and so, on the fourth, as soon as she saw that the guard was fast asleep, she crept out without making a sound. She knew the guard had a tiny lamp on him, sticking out from his pocket. With gentle and swift hands, she carefully took it and noted that he kept snoring.

She knew precisely how to get to the underground system of tunnels with only a short walk outside, but because it was dark, she knew that it would be tricky. She looked up and saw a new moon against a black sky. With slow, quiet, deliberate steps, she made her way into the night. She knew that if she made one false move, her life would be over.

Once she arrived in the tunnels, she turned on the flashlight. She easily found her way to where her shovel had struck the piece of wood a few days earlier. However, she hadn't any tools that night, and she realized the strength in her hands would have to suffice. She dug with a ferocity that she had never felt before. Her hands grabbed furiously at the earth. She thought of her father, whom she had not seen for all this time; she thought of her mother and the sweetness of her smile, the beauty in which she saw the world and the violin she played every evening; she thought of her two younger sisters, who were as delicate as bolts of lace. She dug and gripped the earth as her tears came down.

Her hands, covered in blisters and blood, finally touched upon the wood, and felt its smoothness, worn by the many years spent underground. Grazing the soft, sanded cedar, the earth moved gently under her fingertips, and with ease, she uncovered a small chest. To her astonishment, the latch opened easily.

Slowly and carefully, she lifted the lid and unfolded the blue silken fabric that protected the treasure inside. On the top was a card, with a picture of a single red rose. In Polish, it read: "*To my dear Rahel, my beloved, on our engagement. May we have a lifetime of happiness together. Yours forever. Ibrahim.*"

"Oh, my God. They were Jewish…" Lucia whispered to the earth surrounding her.

Lucia then unfolded the dress, its red dazzling her with light. She held it up and was mesmerized by this vision of brightness, by the rubies that delicately laced the collar, by the folds of silk that sashayed around the contours of the dress.

She gasped. She gently touched the cloth, feeling its softness envelop her. She lost herself in the silk, in its sensuality; her fingertips guided her to an untainted world.

An intuitive warning light suddenly jolted her brain—an inner voice commanded her to return to her hardened self. She became conscious of having to get back to her cot. She quickly folded the dress back into its original home and covered the chest with dirt, making sure it would be easy for her to get back to, yet impossible for anyone else to find. She ran the length of the tunnel back to the opening, hid the flashlight in the soil and with every bit of alertness that she could muster, she made her way back to her cot. She pulled the thin blanket over her head and fell asleep, with only moments to spare before the guard woke up.

The next day, as her shovel dug into the earth, her mind focused only on the red dress. Its softness and the flow of the fabric touched something in her that she had never experienced and elicited a feeling of something left behind and forgotten.

Later that day, as Lucia continued to work, her mind drifted. Although she had no idea where she was, thanks to that love letter, she knew she was probably still in Poland. She also knew with complete certainty that, directly above where she was digging, there was a home that used to be inhabited by a Jewish family. Although it was not cold, she began to shiver uncontrollably with these realizations.

Most of the time she did not even look at the clothes she was forced to wear, but suddenly she glanced down, and stared at the tattered blue and white striped prisoner garb. She smelled the underwear that she could never change, having only one pair. Her menstrual cycle had ceased, her body continually ached, and she was constantly starving. Her life had been reduced to a piece of nothing, digging in the dirt.

She knew that night that she had to return to the dress. Something about it was calling her. The dress was more than a piece of clothing; it allowed her to dream about transporting herself to a world that was not this one.

At midnight, the guard fell asleep again, and she repeated all the steps that had led her to the chest the night before, this time with more confidence in her steps. Uncovering the hidden flashlight, she quickly and silently made her way into the tunnels. With a swift sweep of her hands, she opened the wooden box, and let the smells of the silk, the cedar, and the earth entirely fill her. Her fingers stroked the softness and enveloped the fabric. She pulled the dress completely out of its case and held it to her, imagining a more feminine body fitting into it, being that beautiful Rahel who was loved and cherished, who had an infinite future, who embodied the flow of this perfect design. As she felt the luxuriousness of all that was this dress, she strained her ears and heard something from above. Faintly at first, and then with more bravado, she recognized a violin. It was a recording of Yehudi Menuhin playing the Beethoven violin concerto. She knew this precisely, as her mother played the violin, and many nights she would play this same recording on their gramophone.

Holding up the dress, hearing the music from above, remembering her mother, Lucia began to feel powerful waves of sorrow and joy. She experienced death and life, endings, mixed together with a vague sense of a renaissance that folded around her heart–her young, impression-able, yet already hardened and grieving heart–yearning for peace, for the absolute purity of the violin and a red dress.

The violin stopped playing. The piece was over. Lucia sensed she would never be able to return to this dress again. She grabbed the silk and lace collar and bit hard into it, ripping it out, and quickly, she slipped it in her underwear. She folded the dress and put it back in the chest, that she buried carefully, and rushed back to her cot, again, barely in time before the guard opened his eyes.

The following night, the guard was replaced by a younger one, who never closed his eyes on duty.

* * *

Later that week, out of the corner of her eye, Lucia spotted her father, the first time she had seen him since that dreadful first day. He was no longer the handsome, strong, and muscular man she had known her entire life. Instead, hobbling to his death, looking sick, emaciated, and gaunt, haggard by the life he had been thrown into, her father, led by the guards, dragged one foot and the other to the gas chambers. His gait was a stark expression of the torture of being alive in a time where everything that had once been good had been brutally stolen away.

He glanced up, saw Lucia and screamed out her name. Lucia tried to run to him, but the guards pushed her away. They kept an eye on her, not allowing her one final goodbye. She had to watch him stripped of his dignity, as he walked to his own grave.

The next day more guards pushed Lucia onto a train that was crammed with hundreds of others. It was dark inside and smelled of feces. They were leaving Auschwitz. Throughout the day and into the night, up into the northern regions of Germany, the train rumbled and groaned. They arrived at the entrance to Bergen- Belsen Concentration Camp. It was November 1944, and snow was already covering the ground.

Numb and exhausted, Lucia followed every order. Again, she had no idea what she was digging, perhaps this time it was graves. She did not care. The swath of fabric that she managed to keep in her underwear was the only thing that reminded her of life and hope.

On the morning of the 15th day of April 1945, the locks were re- moved, the sun brilliantly emerged, and in a surreal atmosphere, all prisoners began the slow walk towards freedom.

That afternoon, at precisely 12:01 pm, a large car drove in the gates, stopped, and a young man descended from the passenger seat. He carried a violin case. There, near the entrance to Bergen-Belsen, as former prisoners walked blearily by, smiling and shaken with feelings so powerful that only tears could express, Yehudi Menuhin, violin in hand, began to play.

The freed men and women, looking like skeletons, some barely able to walk, stopped, fell to their knees, and wept, as Menuhin played. He looked in their eyes, and with each turn of his bow, he expressed their sorrow. Yet, with the uplift of each bow stroke, with the major key dominantly played, the E String surging with notes that ascended into a place that could only be called sublime, there was, on that day, a collective feeling of hope. Lucia was a part of all this, as she sobbed. The violin felt so close to her soul, she could kiss each string.

With the music still in her ear, Lucia walked. All around her was the heavy tread of emaciated and ruptured human beings, one step following another, with nowhere to go but out.

Every one of these people had names and histories, most of which had been obliterated, yet they were the remaining few survivors. Some were children, still very young; others had arrived young and spritely and had aged to resemble an old person, straining to take each step. Lucia, now 20, had spent almost a fifth of her life in a concentration camp. She too walked with great effort, her ox-like strength now a part of her past. Her body had taken the form of a middle- aged woman, torn apart and weary.

* * *

She, along with thousands of others ended up in a displaced person camp, back in her home country of Poland. Previously outgoing and talkative, she had become silent and restrained. In the DP camp she felt imprisoned, lost, and truly displaced. She had no home to return to, no family, and her friends of the past could be anywhere, and most probably dead.

One night, in the middle of a bout of sleeplessness, she decided she wanted to start completely over. The next day, she inquired about the possibility of emigrating to Australia. She filled out all the necessary paperwork, which the DP camp took care of, and, in November 1945, as the snow pummeled against her naked head, she boarded a ship. Weeks later, she was one of the first war refugees to arrive in Sydney Harbor. She breathed in the balmy late spring air, tasted the salt on her lips, and knew instantly that she would never leave this new home.

In her first days in Australia, Lucia walked the streets of Sydney in a trance-like state, looking for red. Red was, for her, the color she needed. Lucia became obsessed with all shades of red. Red became the expression of freedom and escape. The image of red, dreams of red, and pictures in red turned out to be hope for her during those first few months, as she adjusted to her new life. Somehow for her, red took away all the rage, the sadness, the facelessness, and all those years where she had experienced the deterioration of the human soul. Red transformed all this, gave her strength and vitality, and pushed aside her previously murdered dreams, allowing her the infinite space to find life again.

Lucia decided, in the beginning of her new life in the Southern Hemisphere, that she would become a seamstress. When she was a child, her mother had taught her how to sew, and somehow, she remembered everything she had learned. After a few inquiries, she was taken on as an apprentice with a dressmaker on the outskirts of town. There, she would spend the next chapter of her life perfecting the art of being a fine tailor. Her life revolved around this new trade. In fact, it was there that she met her future husband.

Gábor, from Hungary, had recently emigrated to Australia from Birkenau. Like Lucia, his entire family had perished there. He entered the building where Lucia was working, asking about a job as a garment maker, a trade he had learned from his father. Lucia was the only one present when he had walked through the door. She had never seen anyone as handsome as this young man. When he introduced himself, her heart skipped a beat as she remembered the red dress, and the note on top–the gift from Ibrahim to his beloved. During those months in her new home, she had consciously erased much of the camp experience. All at once, everything came back to her, a cloud of grey, the horrors of her past, yet somehow the memory of the love of Ibrahim for Rahel, and all that the red dress represented, swam around her head in a dizzying fashion, as she looked at the man in front of her, as she felt, staring into his eyes, that Gábor would propose to her one day, and she wouldn't say no.

The years passed. Some moments were prolonged, some brief. There was love, a definite love, between Lucia and Gábor. They opened their own shop together in the heart of Sydney. They were blessed with children: a boy, Daniel, and a girl, Sophia. They watched them grow up and venture out into the world: one to the UK, and one to America, leaving them alone again, still in love and now almost old.

Their son became a computer scientist, and their daughter, resembling her grandmother in many ways, was a violinist. Sophia often phoned Lucia to tell her about her life and plead with her to come visit her in America. Lucia always said no. She knew she could never leave Australia. She clutched onto this country with a tight fist, knowing that it held her, gave her roots, and that she would stumble if she left.

Her life and her work with Gábor in Sydney were all that she needed, even if not a day went by where she didn't miss her children, especially her daughter.

One day, as Lucia felt her age ominously creeping up on her, she heard on the radio that Yehudi Menuhin would be performing the Beethoven violin concerto at the Sydney Opera House. She bought two tickets, and for the week before this concert, it was all she could think about. On the morning of the event, she had butterflies in her stomach, only thinking of the day he played as she walked out of the barbaric life she had been thrust into.

Lucia held Gábor's hand so tightly that his knuckles turned white, as Menuhin played with a passion that penetrated deep into her heart, and as she remembered the day she held the red dress. When he was finished, she cried and cried, applauding louder than anyone around her. She brought her husband down to the backstage area when the concert was over, and they waited until an old man emerged, striking still in his presence. Lucia moved up to be next to him, to get his attention. She told him, with her hand on his, her memories of him playing Schubert as she was released from Bergen-Belsen, and how his performance that day had transcended that place of horror to the sublime and had affected her whole life. She looked in his eyes, and he looked in hers. They both teared up and let the tears flow, as they acknowledged in that moment humanity and music, and the ability of the latter to reach into a person's soul and embrace life itself in all its beauty.

That night Gábor held Lucia when she cried, when they made love, when they both found peace, as they did together, night after night and day after day. They each wanted to hold onto these moments, to never let go of the goodness they had together.

Yet, they also knew their time was limited. Gábor had been diagnosed with cancer and had just months to live. He told Lucia he did not want to have medical intervention and wanted to die in her arms.

One month before his death, they closed the shop and spent every day together. Lucia tended to Gábor, watched him sleep and breathe until his last breath, slow and deliberate–an exhale that floated into her arms and her heart. Gábor's last breath released in her a pool of tears.

* * *

Their children, neighbors and friends came, a blur in her life as she reminded herself that she was, after all, a survivor. When they all left and the quiet in the apartment on Wallaby Street was interminable, she went to her closet one night and pulled out the ruby, silk and lace collar. She had stored it at the back of all her boxes in the closet, and not even Gábor knew of it. During all those years, she never had the strength to even as much as glance at it. There were many times she almost did, but always refrained, as she would become weak with fear of too many memories that might ensue.

But now, as it lay on the bed in front of her after all those years, the bed that had created her two babies and had held her and her late husband night after night, even in its tattered state, the red silk dazzled her senses. She began to remember the good things–her mother and father, the love in her family, and the life she had before the fateful knock on the door. She remembered every moment of her life with Gábor, the love of her life, and with their children, growing up, day after day. And she remembered Yehudi Menuhin and his violin and the ethereal quality that entered the deepest places of the human heart. Somehow, it was in these memories, and in the redness that did not seem to fade from this fabric, that her own dreaminess stayed alive, that her passion to live and love life could still flourish and survive.

The next day she went to her favorite fabric store, and with saved money she had put behind the box with the ruby collar, she walked quietly in, ready to create the most beautiful dress she had ever made. After a time of perusing everything in the store, touching and stroking fabric after fabric, she emerged a few hours later with a luxurious hand-made red silk from Japan.

Every day she sat at her sewing machine. The design of the dress had never left her memory. As she sat and pressed her foot on the pedal, her hands knew exactly what to do to recreate that genius, sumptuous red silken dress.

One week later, she held up the dress and examined it, admiring her work, knowing that one piece was remaining: the ruby collar. As she stitched it in, her tears began to flow, as she took herself back to the time of her youth. The rubies dazzled, and inspired hope and a will to never give up, to create beauty in all that one can do in life.

She laid the finished dress on the bed and stood back, noting the exactness to the original. As she looked over at her work, she felt a finality surrounding her, her life's work, her own finishing seams, like the ones she created on the silk dress.

The phone rang at that moment. She felt still in her place of reverie but somehow knew it was vital to pick up the phone, as she sensed it was an important call not to be missed. Her daughter spoke.

"Matka. Mama. Minka…." She always gave her mother three derivatives, three terms of endearment when she talked to her.

"You will never guess where I will be next week! I am going to play at Carnegie Hall!!!"

"Oh, my darling!!! That's wonderful!!!!! Oh, my baby!!! And what are you to play?"

"The Beethoven violin concerto. With the New York Philharmonic."

Lucia's mouth dropped. "Oh, sweetheart!!!"

"Oh, Mama. Please come! I got you tickets. A box seat. A flight here."

There was silence on the other end. Somehow Lucia knew she would one day be asked to do this. Everything she had repeated to herself for all these years, that she would never leave Australian soil, dizzied around her head at that moment. Memories and fears flooded her, things she had told herself, stories to keep her safe, as her daughter waited patiently at the other end of the line.

Lucia was silent. They each knew that it would take a boulder to change her resolute decision to never leave her Southern Hemisphere. Yet, each of them also knew that, buried under all the memories and the stories, and the years of maintaining status quo, Lucia had a passion that was insistent, and this passion would dictate to her just one thing: she had to be at that concert.

After this interminable silence, where thoughts reigned over the heart, where entrenched messages gnarled themselves around scraggly branches, Lucia finally saw some light.

She uttered a small, yet distinguishable "*Yes!*".

For forty-eight hours, sleep took over Lucia. In those two solid days in her bed, Gábor came and went, kissing her, holding her, touching her everywhere. He held the red dress, caressing each fold as he did his wife, loving her creation as he loved her. For two days, Lucia felt soothed and nourished by him, by her sleep, and on the third day she awoke and began to pack.

She was going to America.

She put clothes in her suitcase, and then she took them out. In the end, she packed very little, making room for the red dress, for that was all that mattered.

On the plane, she mostly slept. She occasionally looked out the window and then glanced at her watch. She felt disoriented, frightened, yet also exhilarated. This was her first trip on an airplane, her first time over an ocean that spanned endless miles. She thought of Gábor, wanting him there, wanting to feel the softness of his hands in hers, the reassurance that she would be fine, that alone, she could carry on, and that alone, she could return to the Northern Hemisphere.

Right before landing, the plane flew by the Statue of Liberty. When she landed, it was spring, and the soft breezes of New York welcomed her, as she stepped off the plane, and listened to the cacophony of sounds, a hum of life.

At the end of the customs line, there she was, her lovely Sophia, her arms open. The two of them held each other tightly. Each one knew what a monumental event this was, her mother in her arms at JFK airport.

Sophia had booked a two-bedroom hotel suite for the two of them, overlooking Manhattan. Mostly, they just wanted to talk in the common room and capture their lives that they had missed out on for all those years. When Sophia needed to practice, Lucia retired to her room and listened to the brilliance of her daughter's violin. She thought of her own mother, remembering the sounds of her mother's practicing that put her to sleep night after night. Lucia drifted off to a deep slumber as her daughter played and rehearsed the encore she would perform the next evening, one that she had thought about performing for many years.

Around noon the next day, Lucia awoke, famished and giddy. Sophia greeted her with hugs and a huge meal. After breakfast, before her daughter had to begin her mental preparation for her performance, Lucia, still in her night dress, sat next to her, with a silk box in her hands.

"For you, my darling."

Sophia looked at her mother with admiration and tenderness as she took the box and carefully opened it, letting the red silk dress with the ruby collar slip between her hands, as she stroked its luxuriousness. Tears fell from the two of them, mother and daughter, as heads nodded, and they acknowledged the entire story of this dress from the beginning to this moment, and all that it was.

"There are no words, Mama, to express how stunning this dress is. Thank you! You made this after Papa died, didn't you?"

Lucia nodded.

"And you traveled with it all the way from Sydney."

They hugged again and again. That night, there would be a beautiful woman, wearing a dazzling red dress, performing the Beethoven Violin Concerto in Carnegie Hall. And that woman was Lucia's daughter. She beamed at the thought, as Sophia got herself ready, the day passing in a dizzying blur. Later, there was a surprise knock at the door: her son Daniel with his wife Laura and their two children, who had freshly arrived from London, greeted her. With embraces all around, they announced that the limousine was ready outside to take them all to Carnegie Hall.

In a box seat, Lucia sat, surrounded by her entire family, as her daughter entered the stage, and the audience applauded with gusto, ready for her brilliance. Her dress dazzled everyone, as the rubies glistened when she moved, and the folds of her dress sashayed around her body when she performed with a sweetness and a passion that overcame Lucia. She closed her eyes and listened to her daughter's talent. She was overcome with pride. When Sophia performed the solo cadenza, she sensed that mouths dropped in that hall. Lucia felt her own buoyancy as she let the music enter all her wounded places.

When Sophia finished the concerto, she received a dozen standing ovations. When all was quiet, she looked out at the audience and found her mother. While she held back her tears, she told everyone in the audience the entire story of the red dress. When she ended the story, she played, as her encore, the music from *Schindler's List*, composed by John Williams, and first performed by Itzhak Perlman. She invited everyone in that concert hall to stop and reflect, to weep, and to never forget this tragic time in history that begged for music to transcend.

When she stopped, not an eye was dry in Carnegie Hall. Everyone reflected on her red dress and on their own life stories. Finally, after the twentieth curtain call, Sophia walked off the stage.

* * *

A few days later, after celebratory parties and excursions with her family around New York, Lucia was back on the plane, heading home. She was very happy, but completely exhausted. While one hand touched her wedding ring, and the other clutched the program from her daughter's concert, she fell into a deep sleep. Her dreams were filled with a kind of sweetness that sang to the depths of a violin, to the red dress, and to the love of her family.

When she woke up, she stared out the window, and sensed she was somewhere between the hemispheres, in a place of clarity, open to the next stage of her life. She thought about an article her son had given her. The Australian government was looking for Holocaust survivors to team up with Aboriginals who had been a part of the Stolen Generation. They would be collectively talking about their experiences with high school students, sharing their stories, opening secrets, revealing truths in the attempts to create an environment of compassion and tolerance.

Lucia felt energized by this idea. She knew it was time to tell her story, to not just find or make a red dress, but to find in herself all that the red dress represented. As her eyes dreamily focused on myriads of puffy clouds, Lucia sighed.at the thought that now, a new path had begun in her life. It represented a completion... and the beginning... of something not yet tangible. Yet, amid this transition, she experienced on that plane a sense of peace, a feeling of healing, like the breath one savors when one is coming home.

WALKING HOME

Alex drove on the quiet highway from Port Victoria to Adelaide. The sun dipped behind the barren hills; a golden haze surrounded her. She had had a pensive day at the beach looking out at Wardang Island. Every summer during her childhood, her family took a boat there from Point Pierce, to live on untouched land for three months at a time. Nowadays, no boats traveled there anymore.

At 9pm, the South Australian sun lingered on the pavement. The air was heavy with blistering heat.

With her eyes on the road, the asphalt hot and smooth under her tires, her mind drifted to memories and jumbled thoughts, landing on one simple revelation: the bush called her...

A kangaroo suddenly crossed the road, hopping and jumping, leaping in the air, freedom splayed out in its haunches. She almost ran over it; its suddenness stunned her. She swerved to the left to avoid a crash.

"Fucking 'ell!", she muttered to herself as she drove on. She captured her breath, noticing that her heart had skipped several beats. An image of her mother came to her.

She had told her once: "If a kangaroo hops in front of you, keep moving forward and do not look back. Do what you can to avoid hitting the animal. Surge your life ahead, with big leaps, and leave what is hurting you and let the ancestors guide your path."

Back in the suburbs of Adelaide, on a road that shrieked with sound, Alex finally pulled into her driveway. She closed her eyes and sighed. It was too hot to stay in the car, and she got out quickly to get into the cool of her living room. She plopped on the sofa and looked around. She never threw anything out, and her house was full of memories, pieces of existences of her life, some which were long over. She stared at her photos. Most of her family was dead. The framed faces were the reminders of her past, her connection to her land, her culture.

* * *

Later that evening, Lucille, her white girlfriend, knocked on the door, let herself in and curled up next to her on the couch. Alex told her about the kangaroo encounter. Then she cried. They were quiet together as Lucille held her.

The light faded, and as she stroked Alex's hair, Lucille asked: "What is the most salient feature of being Aboriginal?"

Alex answered, in a quiet, yet determined voice: "Survival."

She didn't say another word. Her silence spoke and echoed into the oncoming night, ricocheting off tarnished walls, prisons of the mind screaming to be free.

The TV blared in the background–a news program where white Australians were asked if they knew any Aboriginal people. Most of those interviewed claimed they did not, shrugging their shoulders, escaping their own past, their own rabbit-proof fences, and messages learned along the way.

"Oh, they are always walking somewhere." One woman responded. Her face was blank and hard.

Alex turned off the TV, disgusted.

Lucille took her hand and led her to the bedroom. She lit a candle and slowly took off Alex's clothes. Her tongue playfully slid up and down Alex's skin.

"More. PLEASE do not stop, do not ever stop!", Alex murmured. "I love the way you know me."

The candlelight flickered. Floodgates released water; waves crashed against the promised shore.

Somewhere there was hope.

Somewhere.

* * *

Where are they walking? Why do they walk?

Alex thought about this question the next day, letting her mind wander as she got in her car. She sipped her coke and blasted the A/C, as she cruised through the suburbs.

Except she substituted *they*, for *we*.

She popped David Bowie's *Tonight* in the CD player. The blend of Bowie and Tina Turner's voices came out like warm honey. She let the words and the music of the guitar flood into her ears and clear her mind.

"Everything will be alright..."

She sighed. Everywhere in her mind there were images of her people, the ancient ones lost in the city, bewildered, as they wandered through the streets, looking for a rock to hold onto, to steady them. That weekend, at the Trash and Treasure, as she was looking to buy some runners, one of the ancient ones walked up to her as if in a dream. Her feet were bare. Her hair was un-brushed, matted in all directions. Her clothes were mismatched, a kaleidoscope of colors. Their eyes met for a second that seemed to last several generations. A brief smile, heads nodded and then, in a second, the ancient one turned and disappeared, back to the dream, and wandered away.

If she walks, I walk, she thought. *We are all walking together, connected in spirit. We are all family.*

There is no beginning; there is no end. My people, the oldest living culture on earth; we span thousands of years.

We walk to be free. That is why we walk. We walk until we find our people again; then we stop.

She turned up the volume and let the silky voice of Tina Turner and the suaveness of Bowie's accentuate those thoughts. Tears welled up in her eyes. The ochre earth beckoned her, expanse of open space. The bush called her home.

* * *

"I am leaving you," Alex said quietly, two mornings after that night her lover had stroked the most tender of places inside her.

"Oh my God, Alex! Why?" Her white skin seemed whiter that day under her tank top.

"I have to be with my people."

"Do you still love me?"

"Of course! I will always love you. I just need to go home. I can't live this lie anymore. I have to walk with my people."

"Do you hate me because I am white?"

"No, I will never hate you. You are the reason I feel the need to be free."

"What do you mean?"

"You have loved me like no other white person has ever loved me. And you have shown me that I needed to find my people. I need to go back. I am so lost here, and the older I get, the more I am getting lost. I am dying here, in this city, where there is trash everywhere, where there are remnants everywhere, forgetting who I am!"

"Damn it, Alex, can I go with you?" Tears streamed down her face, as she grabbed the tattooed arm of her lover, and with her finger outlined the print of the name of Alex's deceased niece, as she spread her wet tears up and down her arm. Alex shivered.

She wanted to rip the clothes off this woman who loved her.

Instead, she gently pulled her arm out of Lucille's grip, took her keys from the table, put on her San Francisco Giants baseball cap, and let the screen door slam behind her.

Lucille stood motionless. She stared past the tattered screen door, as the engine turned over, as Alex slowly turned out of the driveway, heading north, away.

* * *

Strip mall after strip mall blurred together that day as Alex drove vowing not to stop. Even her favorite "Cash Converters" did not distract her as she held the wheel in her two hands, propelled to leave the city, drive away from it all and the feelings inside of her, the pain of leaving Lucille like a red brick being thrown at her.

Kate Bush sang in the background. She belted out her innermost thoughts.

"It lay buried..."

Malls gave way to small country shops, and road signs began to disappear. Finally, alone on the open road, Alex began to breathe again.

Sky and land. An abundance of each surrounded her. Her eyes opened. So did her heart. She was always aware of her surroundings, and as she drove, letting the kilometers fuse into each other, she noticed colors, shadings of reds and blues and browns. Her skin burned and became darker from the sun blazing from her open window. On the highway, alone, the bush comforted her. Sand, earth and trees. Spinifex spun webs of home.

Tears flowed down her face as she fixed her eyes on the road, the one that wove itself around hills, sacred land that once held her people. In her mind, she imagined a time just a few hundred years earlier, before the white settlers, when the bush surrounding her housed her culture—brown skin meeting only brown skin. In their eyes, you could taste freedom, the land bordering them, holding them and their dreams.

"Oh, Mum! I miss you." Tears dampened her cheeks as her mother's face came into view.

"You taught me what it is to be Kaurna. You were my link to my people. I am so lost now. I am coming home. I am coming back to my people, back to your spirit and all that was."

"When you died Mum, I forgot who I was. You thought that my niece would look after me, but when she died a few years ago, I became a slippery mass of nothing. I don't even know how to connect with my people. They have all been stolen, Mum. Our culture has been stolen away."

Alex fixed on a memory, one she did not witness, but felt like she had. Her mother, in this vision, was screaming, stamping the ground, dust flying everywhere as her two daughters and her son were stolen away, stolen from her arms, playing one moment and taken the next. No words came out of her mouth, as screams fed screeches of despair, where there is no answer in the night, when the dust settles, when the children are all gone, when there is no hope left.

She wondered, when a culture, when a generation is stolen away, where do you go next? The generations after that become lost in the dredges of a suburban blur, wandering, confused, looking for one's people, a tree to lean against. Humanity becomes muddied, a version of life that has no meaning.

"How did you keep loving, Mum, when everyone was gone? Your children, your people's children? You loved everyone. Everyone loved you. Love became your shield, maybe, a shield against all the rage you must have felt. Or maybe love was all that made sense in a senseless time."

"Every day, Mum, I face people who hate us, who walk away when they see us, who think we are some lowly species. They are the children and the grandchildren of those who stole our people away, my sisters, my brother. They raped the earth and then my people, stealing our pride, and then they wonder why there is so much emptiness, so much drinking. They wonder why we are always wandering. The woman the other day at the market, she was so lost. She looked at me, Mum, and she was searching for someone to hold onto. Abandoned, uncared for. All she needed was to look at me, and then she moved on. So many homeless by the river, getting drunk, passing out in a stupor, they have nowhere to go."

"Why, Mum? How did this happen? You could never get a job like you wanted to. They would never hire you, never give you any respect. And then, they took your children from right in front of you. They grabbed them and shoved them in the back of a truck, while you wailed. Your wailing echoes in my mind, my life, now, always. You, my precious mother."

"You left us too soon. I still need you, Mum."

* * *

Alex inserted another CD. Cyndi Lauper's voice rose up inside her car and echoed across the endless expanses of bush she was driving through.

"If you're lost…"

Was it a mirage? A figure came out of the bush, grey hair, matted, hands wrinkled like a snake's skin ready to be shed, teeth crooked, brown, smiling. A cane to lean on, bent like the back, yet still holding.

Alex slowed to a stop. The air was thick with heat, dry and heavy. The sun burnt down on everything. She turned off the engine and got out of the car. Everywhere, there was quiet, as she looked at the elder, as they stared at each other, gazing into each other's eyes, deep into the soul. The woman nodded and silently reached out her withered hand. Bony bits of flesh sunk into Alex's muscled hand.

"Why have you come? What are you waiting for?"

Yet these were silent questions. There were no words, just gestures. Nods, and then the tears, small, at first, then bigger. The storm brewed inside; sadness and rage jumbled together like rain and thunder.

"I have been away."

"Yes."

The two women embraced. Alex shook while the old woman cooed.

Then, the elder told her a quiet and gentle story, in an ancient language, her coos tenderly filtered through the words. She took her arms and danced them sweetly in the air, like a small bird flying. Then they landed, she pointed to Alex's heart and nodded. Her arms returned to the embrace, as Alex sunk in, sighed deeply, and did not let go while time stood still, and spinifex waved in the warm breeze surrounding them.

Something got stirred in Alex, something significant, where she got taken to the edge of the bush where the outback meets the sea, to the edge of all she knew. She closed her eyes, the woman's arms still around her. There was *The Dreaming*. Her ancestors appeared from all directions. The cooing of the old woman turned into a chant, and the louder the chant, the more the spiritual world came alive. They circled around Alex and the elder, while the day turned into night and the Milky Way, like a giant river, enveloped them in its luminous embrace. The spirit world created images in the landscape, forms, shapes and beings while the warm breeze mingled with the brilliant stars in the night sky. Guttural cries blended and created a tapestry of sound and a feeling of mainly love.

During this time the sky had darkened. Thick clouds quickly emerged from all directions, accompanied by an energizing wind that gave strength to the beginnings of light raindrops. The brilliant stars clouded over, the quickly passing storm gained force, and the winds twisted and turned. The sound of the rain brought new life. Alex looked up and around, grabbing raindrops on her tongue, in the folds of her neck, as she and the old woman knew, that the renaissance of her spirit with her people had begun.

Water, they chanted, in an ancient language. They pointed in the direction of the sea, and nodded their heads as the wind calmed, and the drops of water softened to nothing. The storm was over.

Alex embraced the elder one last time. She felt tears on her cheeks, coming from the both of them. They blended into a soft fluid, a healing balm to a grieving soul. Back in her car, she listened to the purr of the engine as she drove through familiar land, the bush on either side, the sea beckoning her soul.

A grove of ghost gum trees lined the highway. The stark white bark contrasted with the red earth, a simple reminder that she was home, that she had arrived in Whyalla. She could drive this stretch with her eyes closed. Past a few strip malls and the city center, she drove to the limits of what was her town, to the Spencer Gulf, to the sea. She pulled into a car park and smelled the salt in the air. She felt her mum's spirit around her. She loved this place, this quiet beach, water that bathed all her troubles away. When she was a child, Alex would come here often with her mum and her favorite niece. The three would laugh and laugh until night fell. Fishing from the pier, they would usually catch a strong fish or a king George whiting. Her mum would pull out the al foil, and they would make a fire. They would roast their delicate catch until it was done. Each bite tasted like pure love.

Alex heard her niece and her mum that night. Their voices echoed in her head as she looked out along the pier that stretched for what appeared to be miles and miles. The warm night breeze touched her skin in a tender caress. Walking slowly down the smooth, worn wood, the heaviness in her heart began to lighten as she felt no longer alone. At the end, she stopped and looked out. The familiar expanse of endless water embraced her. From her pocket, she pulled out two small brown paper bags, one with "Mum" written on it, the other with "S". She put the "Mum" bag back in her pocket as she opened the "S" bag. Her hand reached in and felt the softness, the lightness of what remained of her niece. She heard her laughter, memories of so many years of enjoying life, as she grabbed the handful of ashes and sprinkled them into the cool water. She watched the waves absorb the fine dust into its folds. As Alex emptied the contents of the bag into the water, a shooting star streaked across the sky. She could feel the ancestors dance with honor accepting her offering, this connecting piece of flesh to spirit, housed in the safety of the sea.

Next, she pulled out the "Mum" bag, and years of memories flashed before her eyes. Alex was the lucky one, born after the era of the stolen children, a child brought into this world with the hopefulness of a new generation, the child that her Mum would never have to watch being ripped out of her tender grasp. Her mum had transferred her feelings of rage into delight, and Alex received love in its purest form. When her mum got sick at an early age, Alex shriveled up inside, yet cared for her night and day, wanting to be the one who could save her from decline. After two years, she succumbed to cancer. At her funeral, there were hundreds, coming from all over Australia to pay their respects to a woman who had loved anyone in her path, sometimes even creating paths to those who needed love.

Alex never encountered a day when she did not long to have her mother return to the world of the living. She reached into the bag, taking the ashes and letting them bathe her hands, the wetness of the tears sticking to them like glue. She did not want her mother to ever leave. She wanted the ashes to sink into every pore of her skin. She took a handful and raised it to the sky, remembering a blessing her mother had taught her in the ancient language, praying out loud as she felt her mother all around her.

"Mum. You are everywhere, inside of me in the spirit world, in these ashes, in the sky itself."

Her fingers opened slowly and gently. Alex heard in her mind her mum's joyous screams as she gave birth to her, at home, that day so many years earlier She saw her mum crying with joy when she held her youngest in her arms and whispered to her that no one would ever hurt her or take her away, that she would be there always to protect her, that love would always surround this little girl held in her arms. Alex remembered her mum looking straight into her eyes, the day she was to leave this earth, telling her beloved daughter to love someone, to love someone fully and cherish them forever. Her entire body shook, she wildly felt her mother's presence in her as she held the last bit of ashes in her hand and sensed the power of these final words. Quickly, the ashes flew up and swirled around her in a fiery haze, momentarily blinding her, until they floated effortlessly into the inviting whirling waters below.

Alex peered out to sea, and sensed the earth meeting with the water, her mother moving with the waves, the current taking the last tangible pieces of her away while keeping her spirit safe to float with and join the protective folds of the ancestors. A weight lifted from her heart, the same that the doctors said was suffering, that she would always suffer from, and that might even kill her one day. In the end, as she watched the waves ceaselessly swirling, coming and going, and she finally released the part of her mother she had been coveting for so many years, suddenly, she began to breathe freely. All at once her inhale and her exhale felt effortless, the first time she had experienced this since the day her mother had passed.

She looked up into the sky, gazing at the stars, and noticed that they seemed brighter that night, dazzling, almost blinding, a sign from her people, the ones who had already left but who were always there, guiding her, illuminating her path in everything she did, especially now.

Alex, pockets now emptied, stepped into her car and drove the mile down the road to the yellow house that she knew so well, where she had cried and slept, and had gotten drunk and sick, and had always come back to when she needed to be reminded of family. It was late, and she did not know if her sister was awake, but she saw a light in the bedroom, so she knocked. Her sister recognized the four little knocks. Then silence. Then three short knocks. Opening the door, Lily opened her arms wide, and Alex fell into them, breathing in the familiar and comforting scent of her oldest sister, a musty smell mixed with garlic and lavender.

"Come and sleep. I haven't seen you for months. You are exhausted, I can tell. I have to work in the morning. Sleep, sweetie. You will be here in the evening when I get back?"

Alex nodded to confirm.

They parted ways. Lily pattered down the hall to her room; Alex trudged off, with heavy steps to her long familiar room with blue wallpaper.

She fell asleep within two seconds of hitting the pillow, a sound dreamless sleep that kept her motionless until 5pm the next day. When she awoke, she felt something different in her body. Although she had missed two doses of her heart medication, she felt her lungs beating normally, her breath regular and even. She edged out of the bed with light steps, dancing to the loo, like she did when she was a child. She picked up the package of tablets, stared at them for a second, and one by one popped them out of the foil wrapping and tossed them in the toilet. With a determined smile on her face, she pressed the flusher and watched them swirl away in the vortex of water.

She then stepped into the shower and let the hot water pour onto her skin, soap and shampoo mixing with grime, as she lathered until the remnants of her past flowed from her body and down the drain. She felt rejuvenated afterwards. Her life became one clear spot in front of her.

Her sister brought home a roasted chicken from Woolworth's – Alex's favorite–and together they sat down and ate. Lily talked endlessly about this and that, as she always did. There was a pause, a definite full stop, and she looked into Alex's eyes.

"So, I just found out that there is little cottage for rent, right on the bluff, a mile from here. It might need a little work, but I told the landlord you might be interested. It's very sweet inside. Has everything you need and the most amazing views. I never told you, but Mum left just you an envelope of money: $3000. It's not much, but you can use it to pay the fees to move in, if you like the place. I can help you with the payments after that, until you get settled.

And oh, I just got this in the mail yesterday. It's a scholarship application for the drug and alcohol counsellor training program you were interested in. If you qualify, they can pay 100% of your tuition. It's a yearlong program, and it will start this autumn. The deadline to apply is next week. Upon graduation, they guarantee they will place you in a job position working with our people, earning $30 an hour."

Alex sat speechless. She stared at her older sister, hearing in her mind the story she had heard from her parents, those screams when Lily was seven, way before Alex was born, being stolen from their mother. Her younger sister and brother all looked to her for help that day, and she couldn't do anything, letting all the screams envelop her as all three were yanked from their mother's arms.

She looked at her hardened face, yet softened by life, age, and embraced by her people who always surrounded her at work. Her sister belonged to something greater than her. Somehow, she had managed to smooth out everything that was ugly from her past.

Alex saw her own life swim in front of her, as she reached over and pulled her sister to her, kissing her cheek. She felt her tears moisten the rough dark skin of this woman who adored her, who always had, who was told by their mother, on her deathbed to always keep one eye open for her knowing she just might need it.

The next day she went over to the cottage, and instantly fell in love with this home, overlooking the ocean, a garden to tend in the back, a place to feel the spirit of her mother.

And a place to love and be loved.

She called the landlord and agreed to meet him the next day and sign the papers.

* * *

Getting into her car, she put on Pat Benatar, blasting the music, letting the curves of the road accompany the sway of her body, feeling each beat.

"We belong to the light…"

She raced down the highway, heading south, towards Adelaide. The landscape blurred as she turned on the AC, thinking that only one thing was missing that would make the picture complete. One thing she realized she wanted more than anything else.

The big city loomed in sight, expanses of cement that no longer, and really never did have any meaning to her. Smiling, she drove to the café where Lucille worked.

Walking in, she looked at the gorgeous woman behind the counter, making espressos. It was a different kind of staring, a seeing and a knowing that this was the woman she wanted to spend the rest of her life with.

Lucille looked up and blushed. Alex walked towards her with a zest in her steps. Their eyes locked for a second.

She whispered to a co-worker to take over for a few minutes, as she walked out of the café into the car park. Alex took her into her arms and kissed her there, feeling every bit of her body and soul longing for this woman with dark eyes and the loving heart.

"Come with me to Whyalla! I have a home waiting for us, overlooking the sea and a possible scholarship to the program I told you about. Come with me! We can have a life together, a community, a future. You can have the garden you have always wanted!"

"Yes! Yes!! I have been waiting for you to ask me this! When?"

"Now!"

Lucille motioned to Alex to wait a moment.

She walked into the café, took off her apron, and hung it up, whispering to her co-worker that she loved her job, but she was done, and she was now stepping into her future. Whilst the other woman stared at her, mouth open, Lucille calmly walked out of the Point No Point Café into the waiting arms of the woman who was standing in the car park. Alex felt a warm glow flow gently through her, happy feet dancing to the moon and back.

In her ear, her mother's distinctive voice, whispered:

"Good on ya!"

Alex whispered back, silently, clarity pulsing through her like a rain-soaked river, flowing into the awaiting sea.

"Yeah, Deadly."

ODE TO JOY

I suppose you want me to tell you a bit about myself. I can start with the stereotypes. Most people seem to relate to this way of describing people. Then, after you get all these labels in your head, you can do what you want with them as I tell you who I really am and the rest of my story. I think you might find this one quite interesting. At least I do.

I am queer, or if you have more refined ears, I am lesbian. I am a deaf lesbian. I am not an in-your-face kind of *dyke*, but I am not a doormat, if you get what I mean. I have spent much of my life as a farmer, mostly with sheep, and I love it. I am quite strong. I guess that comes from lifting sheep, birthing sheep, making fences and everything you need to do to take care of them. Maybe one day I will write a short story about keeping sheep. You might be interested. But then again, you might not, so I will keep to my original story that you will probably be more curious about, the one which is not so much about sheep.

I am Canadian, which, in itself, is already a bit of a stereotype, especially for you Americans. I am from Alberta, outside of Calgary, if that means anything to you. I grew up liking big things. What can I say? Where I come from, everyone does. Big land, big open space. Big sky at night. Big homes for big families. Big ideas. If you are from British Columbia, you may think of us as rather slow and dim-witted. More stereotypes.

So, you might be wondering how I came to be deaf. I wasn't born that way. In fact, I had the best hearing in my whole family: I could hear a pin drop. Really, my family used to joke about this, and drop pins in the house, and I'm not exaggerating. I would hear them fall.

So anyway, I was destined to be a farmer—according to my family—but like many kids, I had a rebel adolescent streak in me, and I yearned to become a firefighter. I wanted to save people, homes, cats and dogs and be a hero in my hometown. There weren't any female firefighters where I came from, so there you go. I signed up, passed my coursework, and there I was, in uniform, putting out fires and being important in my town. My family was quite proud of me, and I found some cute girls who thought I was something. I liked that part. Let's face it. Firefighting is much more seductive than farming.

One day, in the middle of the night I was called on duty—not my regular shift, but it was a big fire. An old lady on the outskirts of town. Everyone knew her. Everyone loved Old Mabel, and of course her old dog, Riddle.

Her husband had just died, and her son, a sketchy kind of guy, was supposedly taking care of her. But he was off drinking that night. Mabel was having a hard time being without her late husband, but I don't think she told her son much of this. That night, she got confused and left the stove on in the kitchen. Not long after, the house burst into flames.

There was so much clutter in the house. Before he died, her husband—already in his old age—hadn't removed the paint cans and other flammables accumulated in the basement. I ran inside; the house seemed hotter than I had ever encountered. I had to find Mabel.

She was lying on her bed, barely breathing, and flames were everywhere. I grabbed her and literally threw her out the window to the trampoline in the expert hands of my colleagues. Then I remembered the dog and searched for him in the house. I finally found him in the basement, huddled in a corner, whimpering and looking up at me with a tragic "please get me out of here" look. I did manage to carry him in my arms and threw him out the window like his cherished mistress. It was my turn to get out, but I tripped over the cluttered floor of the basement floor, and my foot got trapped. The flames began to engulf me. I heard cracking noises everywhere, and explosions in my ear.

The amazing part of this story is that, somehow, I dislodged my foot and stumbled up and out of the window. I managed to survive without any burns on my body, as I was fully covered in gear. I knew my foot was broken, but after I jumped out the window and was caught by my buddies, I sensed something was wrong besides it. The ambulance for Mabel had left, and another one was on its way for me. I had gone unconscious. Later, in the hospital, they discovered I had lost ninety-five percent of my hearing in both ears.

Because of this, the doctors signed a paper that now forbids me to be a firefighter. At first, I was super angry. At least I had farming to return to after my foot healed.

They say that the Albertans are rather superhuman. So here is the superhuman part of my life. I am not making any of this up, and so many people have told me I need to tell my story, so I continue...

I have got to go back a bit to my life to fill you in. When I was a tiny kid, my mum and I went to see "*The Sound of Music*" at the local theatre. I fell in love with Julie Andrews—I was already a dyke in train-ing of course. But, also, there was a live orchestra playing, and when I wasn't gawking at Julie Andrews, I was staring at the violins. I loved the sound they made. I asked my mum what instrument it was, and when she answered, I told her I wanted to learn to play the violin. It turns out, in my school, they were teaching violin. So, I started learning.

I got pretty good quickly. They said I had perfect pitch. I played all through high school. Also, I composed. I wrote symphonies and string quartets, and the high school orchestra played them. I got trophies and awards many times. Somehow along the way, I stopped playing the violin, though, as I became much more interested in composing.

Let's fast forward in time and go back to the moment of my accident. I recovered from the damage of the fire, except for my hearing. But that didn't stop me. In fact, at that moment, I decided to become a queer Beethoven. I was going to compose symphonies and string quartets and not let my deafness get in the way.

You might have heard how Beethoven composed his symphonies while becoming deaf. And that he was completely deaf in the end. He literally heard the music, the entire score in his head, each note, each instrument, each phrasing. His head was pulsing with sound. He knew music like his own breath. I can't call myself brilliant like he was, but I do know what he must have experienced, at some level, because I too can hear notes and instruments, and because I have played music and composed for so many years, I have music in my head. In a strange way, being deaf has put music even more in my mind than ever before.

For many years, my life revolved around tending sheep and writing music. I can say I was truly happy, except for one thing. I felt kind of trapped, like I knew I couldn't stay in Alberta taking care of sheep the rest of my life, alone, and I knew that somewhere else was calling me.

Do you know how it is, when you have reached the end of the road, and there is no other path, or road or highway, then you kind of scream out, not really, but in your mind for the next avenue...and then one opens to you? It's kind of simple how that happens–it happened to me.

One day, a letter arrived in the mail. It was from the Vancouver

Symphony Orchestra. In the letter, they asked me to compose a piece for their upcoming concert. I sat in my living room, holding this letter, stunned, yet also kind of excited, because it felt like I could do this. How fun… Before I began to wonder how in the hell they knew about me, my friend Linda texted me asking if I had received anything in the mail from VSO. She included a giggle emoji as she told me she mentioned my story to them, and they said they would contact me. I laughed, and thought "Oh yeah, pity on the deaf dyke! You know Vancouver is so utterly PC, and it will look quite good for their PR if I get on the bottom of the program for one of their extra concerts."

I emailed them, and, for the next two months, every waking moment I was not shoveling sheep poo, I was composing a symphony for the VSO. I decided to score it with every single instrument, to make it a grand coming-out party for the entire orchestra and give everyone a part to play. It would be called *Fireworks*, and even the marimba would have a major part. I did not communicate with anyone during those two months. I was literally in a trance, feeling each note and blending it to the entire piece of music. When I finished, I was spent and knew that it was the best work of music I had ever created.

I put the score in an envelope and went to the post office first thing in the morning. Then I went to sleep for two days, letting my neighbors feed my sheep, because I couldn't do a damn thing. I felt so comatose.

A week later, I got an email from the conductor himself. He was so elated he sounded like he was going to combust right there on the computer screen. He not only liked the piece, but he LOVED it, he said. I was pretty darn happy, but sheep were waiting for me, and I felt rather distracted by them that day. I was still thinking I was a pity case, but what the hell, he liked it and that was rather nice for the ego. He gave me the details of the concert that was happening in one month. I sat there staring at his message, knowing that in thirty-one days I was going to be in Vancouver where my piece would be played, although I wouldn't be able to hear it.

My friend Linda had planned to go with me, and she helped me find something decent to wear—something composer looking. We ended up with slacks and a vesty thing that made me look rather chic. I looked at myself in the mirror in the dressing room, and I didn't look bad at all, if I say so myself.

We flew out on Air Canada. We didn't drive; we were both a bit too nervous and not great at the wheel. We got a taxi from YVR airport, which seemed so utterly posh and extravagant. From there we got to the Chan Centre for the Performing Arts, a gorgeous state-of-the-art theatre right on the waterfront with amazing views of the mountains. I stepped out of the taxi to a barrage of photographers, pointing their gizmos right at me. The news cameras engulfed me, and the interviewers had questions upon questions. I looked at Linda, who obviously set this whole thing up and she gave me this nonchalant shrug, letting herself off the damn hook, while I, the shy one, had to tell all the kind, but insistent, media people my story. Now here's the thing; because it's Canada, every one of the questions was signed, and after translated, so hands were going back and forth in all directions. I kind of teared up inside, but caught myself before it showed, so the whole world, or at least Canada, wouldn't see a blubbering composer stepping out of a taxi.

As we entered the concert hall, I was followed by an entourage of probably the entire deaf community in BC. I was stunned. I hardly knew any other deaf people, and here they were, hundreds of them, wanting my autograph. I felt like Alice in Wonderland and wondered if I was on a drug-induced trip or something, heading into a rabbit hole of mysterious goodness. I looked back at Linda who smiled and let me enjoy all the attention that was being showered all over me.

In the middle of all these people there was this woman. I couldn't tell if she was deaf, or just knew how to sign like a dancer, but she was drop dead gorgeous. She winked at me, and, out of all the people there who were giving me all this attention and praise, she was the one who made me feel like I couldn't stand up on the two feet I was born with. She came up to me and gave me a piece of paper with her email address on it. Her name was Lisette, and she was all I thought about as I was sitting in my box seat and the symphony performed Beethoven, Elgar, and Mahler, according to the program. There was an intermission.

And then they played my piece at the end of the concert.

There was a hush in the hall. I felt it in my pores as the conductor came out on stage, put his baton on the stand, turned around and began to speak.

With an ASL translator, he told the audience my entire life story. Even the sheep got mentioned. And the old lady I rescued in the house, so many years ago. He told everyone every little detail I have just told you, and I wept. I only looked at the conductor, but I could sense there were a lot of other people crying at that moment. He turned around, nodded to the orchestra, and they played the first note of my piece, a quiet entrance into the night.

The orchestra was fully into the performance of this piece. I watched them sink into all the nuances I had envisioned, and on every one of the musicians' faces, there was an expression of delight, an exuberance. I could not physically listen to the notes, but I did hear every one of them in my head. I was overcome with this immense joy as

I felt the music I had composed fill the concert hall, reaching every ear in the audience. When it was done, when the fireworks had exploded into a million dazzling lights inside all of us, there was a pause, and then people clapped and waved their hands in the air. Everyone stood up for fifteen minutes afterwards. The conductor had me leave my seat and descend onto the stage and then flowers of all kinds, colors and sizes floated up in the air, landing at my feet.

I looked up into the crowd and closed my eyes. I wanted to remember this day forever, so even if I ended up with Alzheimer's, I still would always have this image in my brain: hundreds of people waving their hands, all standing up in celebration of music, of something I had done that was worthy of praise and recognition.

Vancouver stunned me in its generosity, in its outpouring of graciousness. The deaf community serenaded me with accolades and propositions. Everyone wanted me to get the hell out of Alberta and join them, exploring fully my gift, they said, in composition. I had offers of everything I could possibly have wanted. At the end of too many glasses of champagne, I was feeling as light as a piccolo, ready to elevate into the stratosphere. Finally, the doors began to close, and everyone drifted out into the sweet night. There she was again, waiting until the last person had finished surrounding me. There she was, glowing with a brilliance and sumptuousness that I had never encountered.

Lisette.

With a combination of elation and champagne and a desire that flooded all my senses, I stared into her eyes, that gazed back at me, our longing meeting each other's. I looked deep into her dark eyes and landed there like a bee, finding its source. I pulled her face to mine, and gently grazed my lips upon her cheek, as I met my lips upon hers. I was enraptured by her.

Stroking her hair, I watched her sign. Her hands danced. She told me she had to leave, to catch a flight to Newfoundland that night, and had to rush off. Her face showed me she wanted more, and I signed back I would email her, and that I wanted to see her again. She left and disappeared into the balmy evening. Her taxi sped off as I stood on the sidewalk, mesmerized by her, the entire evening, the next path in my life.

My guardian angel, Linda, was patiently waiting for me and smiling, a witness to everything that happened. She signed she just knew that my stars had all aligned that night.

So, what do I tell you after that? The door opened that night, and the rest of my life kind of just went flowing along. I kept smiling from that day on, knowing that something magical had hit me, knocking me on the head, telling me what I was supposed to do with my life to really be happy.

I got back to Alberta and sifted through the memories of that evening. In my email, I got dozens of proposals, commissions and job offers. I smiled, reading through all these letters. But the one email I was waiting for was Lisette's, a week later. She wanted to see me again. She wondered if I wanted to come and visit her farm on Bowen Island, right across from West Vancouver. She had a house there. She added a PS saying she spins wool from local sheep.

I recognized her name and did a google search to find out she was a writer of fiction, having published several best-selling novels. She was a favorite on Canadian shelves. I also learned that her mother was deaf, and that Lisette's first language was ASL. It said that she taught sign language in the West and North Vancouver School districts. That Google is amazing. I emailed her back, two seconds after I got this information, and then booked a flight for the following week. I was ready to return to Vancouver, to meet again the woman of my dreams, who signed like an angel, wrote books, and lived on a farm, spinning wool for sheep.

Already my life had decided itself. I gave the farm to Linda and her husband, who, for years, had subtly given me hints about how much they loved it. And then I left Alberta for good.

From the proceeds of my commissions, I bought several prize sheep for Lisette. We are living happily, crazily in love with each other.

I compose music for Vancouver, for the deaf community, for the world. There are no limits.

* * *

I thank you for reading my story, but it is not just about me, even if I have done the telling. I believe it is about any one of us who dreams ourselves out of challenges, humbling ourselves, so that others can see our beauty, when perhaps we cannot see it ourselves. And I thank Ludwig van Beethoven, who gave me the inspiration to create music out of deafness, to hear music when the world says there is silence. For truthfully, silence is subjective, and music transcends any barrier. There is an eternal "Ode to Joy" in this declaration, and I am just a witness to all that.

Listen to his ninth symphony, if you don't already have it in your head, and you will know exactly what I mean.

FORTY SHADES OF LIFE

From the hillside where I sat observing the landscape, colors enveloped me everywhere that day. Blue from the sky, white from her dress with inlaid pearls in silk; grey from the ruins of the 1000-year-old castle, each stone telling a story; rust and amber, from the rocks on the shore, weathered by generations of tides and sands; and of course, green, forty shades of green all around us, for this was Ireland.

Everywhere, fields of Ireland surrounded the guests, the bride, the groom, and the birds flying overhead. The lushness of Ireland enveloped them. In the union of these two souls there was freedom, a luminescence, two lives together like a poem that echoed in the wind, the ever-comforting wind from the Atlantic Ocean.

"Boi veshalom ateres baahah gam b'simcha vu 'tzahala, toch emunei am segulah, boi, challah, boi challah shabbas maklesa..."

The cantor sang as the rich smells of earth wafted around us. The train of her dress was lifted by her sisters and aided by the winds. His kippah was firmly placed on his head, and hers was adorned with lavender and shamrock.

"Come in peace, O bride, the Sabbath queen.

Starlings, hundreds of them, their agile bodies choreographed by
only instinct, swirled in the sky above us. In unison, we all looked up,
marveling at the perfection of nature that blended with the sweet melodic harmonies of the Hebrew song of love and devotion.

As daisies and buttercups danced in the breeze around us, we witnessed
a consecration of a marriage, one person to another, Czechoslovakia to
Ireland, a heart to another heart. Ishmael and Talia were newcomers, still
speaking their native Czech; their dark hair distinguishing them, while
love unfolded around us. Gone was a division among people and ideas of
religious persecution as eight men stepped out. They laughed and showed
off their muscles as they grabbed two chairs and instructed the couple to
sit on each of them, as they lifted them in the air. Accordions and violins,
laughter and clapping mingled with the crashing waves of the sea, as tradition wafted around us: theirs, ours, while the newness of the land for was
embraced by the love of our community, our Ireland.

*   *   *

I felt like I knew this couple all my life, and yet I only met Ishmael
the night before, at the local pub. We talked for hours, or rather, I listened to him. In his fragmented English, over pint after pint, I heard
bits and pieces that came together in a haunting, but finally joyous tale
that I had to write down, remember, and share.

It wasn't always a celebration, there weren't always accordions and
violins harmonizing with waves, or a community celebrating them,
honoring love.

"First it was the war," he mumbled, eyes cast down. "There were children, so many children, orphaned in an instant. Have you heard of Kristallnacht?" he asked me.

He continued. His language had spaces and words left out, and I listened carefully, not wanting to miss anything.

One chilly autumn day in 1938, thousands of children saw their parents taken away in an instant. Mass evictions were followed by gunshots, so many that these children, years later, would shudder when a firecracker would explode and they would again be reminded of death. Some of these children would end up in concentration camps. They trembled in the night, waiting for something.

"Ah! The stories in their heads... endless."

I had to concentrate on this next part of the story, as he put his hand on my shoulder and moved me forward, and propelled me into the next theme: hope. His face lit up as he spoke, illuminated by and only by hope. His words were fragmented, yet the meaning was one of survival.

"After the war," he continued, "thousands Czech children wandering, wandering, wandering in orphanages, hidden in homes, convents, anywhere."

Facilitated by a nun in one of the orphanages, these children had written a book. This book made it to England, and to the hands of a man named Rabbi Solomon Taussig. He cried reading these stories of children who had no parents, who were living in a ghostly reality, yet continued to dream of a life without strife. This Rabbi was known for his fearless rescue of Jewish children during and after the War. He looked everywhere for these children, the hide and seek children they were called, whose locations were often ambiguous, whose names and identities were often obscured.

There was a story in this collection about a butterfly, its mystical transformation, the colors of the wings translucent and vibrant, taking flight, leaving behind it's connection to the earth, to the world of bombs and guns and camps, a world which did not make sense, and instead finding a castle far away in the countryside, safe there among the rushes and the forget me nots. In this story the butterfly became free, and thus so did that child.

It was at this moment that the Rabbi decided that he would find this child, and ninety-nine others, and find a castle, perhaps in Ireland, where the children could be safe.

I stared at Ishmael, knowing that he was one of these hundred children.

He went on, with an insistence in his tone. His words were even more fragmented, and I had to work hard to piece together his riveting story.

The Rabbi wrote letters day and night, hundreds of them, in his desperate desire to uncover, to play this game of hide and seek, to locate those children, those one hundred children. For every letter he wrote, he received dozens of lies, misinformation; identities and locations were kept concealed. War changes minds and hearts to bring out fear and often the worst in humanity.

Then, letters started pouring in, from Czechoslovakia, a country he loved, where he did his studies. One hundred children, his children, had been found. They were discovered in attics, cellars, convents, orphanages, behind lampposts that had ceased to function, in the woods, hidden amongst the wild birch forests, underground in the bowels of the city, and in the spaces of the lost and neglected.

And then, there were the encounters, dozens of them. How would they come? Where would they go? Who would take care of them? How would all this be financed? Always with hope, the Rabbi talked, cajoled, promised, and always stood his ground, never for a minute letting go of his dream. At first the Irish government gave its approval, then changed its mind, before giving the green light again, but only for a period of fifteen months. Fifteen months, however, was fifteen months. A castle in Ireland, just as the child had envisioned. Alone, the Rabbi arranged for transport, money, teachers, and nurses to care for these children day and night.

When it was all arranged, the night before he was to leave for Czechoslovakia, the Rabbi held his wife, or rather, she held him, in bed, as he wept.

I wondered how Ishmael knew this piece of information. Did he make it up? Did he make all of this up? As I continued to listen, it didn't seem to matter what was fact and what was fiction. It was his story. And I was the listener, riveted for the next words. He took a breath, drank some more, and continued. I relaxed into his story, waiting for the next part.

Six months after the Rabbi read the story of the butterfly, one hundred children—between seven and sixteen years of age, shoes filled with holes, dirt covering their tattered clothes, faces drawn and gaunt, yet eyes open, hopeful— stepped off the bus on the grounds of Clonyn Castle, in Delvin County, Westmeath, Ireland.

Instantly they wanted to run, for it was late spring, and fields of buttercups and daises beckoned them. Dancing in the cool breeze, two hundred legs ran free, jumping, skipping, hopping, dancing, twirling, feet as light as the wind. Somersaults and cartwheels accompanied by laughs and cries of delight and joy, a child's music, universal in dreams and a love of life. Shoes were thrown off, and the worn leather met the ground with a gentle thud as naked toes grabbed the earth, holding onto it with a sense of complete abandon. Years of suffering and loss were forgotten as the still damp earth squished between their toes and life pulsed back into their blood.

It was hard not to see a glimmer in Ishmael's eyes as he described this last part, his own dream fulfilled, perhaps. It made me wonder if he was the child who had visioned the castle, who inspired this whole story. The glimmer never left his face as he continued.

With the Rabbi at their head, a line of adults– women and men from England–stepped off the bus too, watching, crying, witnessing the fulfillment of their own dream. They could all notice what happens when you release what needs to come out, when you give hope to a child whose hope had been threatened, when you give life to that butterfly whose future depends on its liberation from the cocoon.

They watched the shoes fly, the swirling of bodies dancing to the rhythm of their own joy. They observed the tiny and the bigger ones, the ones who had witnessed horrors, the ones who never got to say goodbye to their mothers and fathers, the ones who saw cousins and siblings die, the ones who almost died themselves. They felt every one of them come to life, like wilted flowers that are finally, finally, given water.

The seventeenth century castle illuminated this life. As day slowly turned to the beginning of night, it was time to put the shoes on, time to take a breath, to hold another's hand, or not, and step into the old building that would become home.

Their futures were uncertain, and nothing could bring back their parents. Very few of them would ever again call Czechoslovakia their country. But children live in the present moment, and for each one, a story had begun in their head, a story that would forever live inside their brains. For in that moment that each child stepped over the threshold into Clonyn Castle, a new stage of their lives surrounded them. The expressions on their faces were riddled with mixtures of excitement, fear and tenuousness, boldness, joy, relief and adventure. Some of the children were deeply conscious of each of these first steps, yet like children, many embodied it with a sense of carelessness, and bounded in with as much exuberance as they somersaulted outside.

Again, my storyteller took a large swig of beer, a deep breath, a pause in the story, as I sensed another very important part was coming up, and he could not wait to tell me all about it. I saw in his eyes that something beyond even hope was about to emerge in his words.

"Listen to next part!" Ishmael exclaimed, his hands touching mine. His palms were sweaty, and his smile took over his face, an impish kind of smile.

The children were expected to do their studies, and they followed a rigorous routine every day, but underlying all the high standards was a sense of joy and freedom to be themselves. For some, there was freedom even to grow up and explore the sensations of being an adult.

One Sunday afternoon, in the heart of the summer, when rain turns to sun in an hour, a teenage girl sat underneath a magnificent mulberry tree, reading a book. Talia was her name. The day before she had just turned eighteen. She had hair as dark as the crow and her eyes were piercing. A look of assuredness encompassed her exterior. Beyond the surface, though, she housed a timidity, a shyness that met her books. She was always reading; always hidden behind the loftiness of the words she pored over.

And here, my storyteller stopped, smiled at me and winked. Always in the third person, he told his story. I never could figure out why he did this. I was entranced by his story as much as the way he told it. I nodded, acknowledging his grand entrance into his own story.

That day, the day after her birthday, a young man, as tall as the rushes around him, approached her with a small box tucked under his arm. This boy, barely a man, with a smile that stretched the span from Ireland to Czechoslovakia, had admired this Talia from the day they were on that bus.

Talia, always reading, never noticed that the boy sitting across from her and down the aisle spent a good part of that day watching her, stunned by her beauty, by her concentration, by every aspect on her face as she read. Her expressions told a story, and he memorized them, so that when he lay on his bed that night, he relived her face in his mind, her story lulling him to a sweet sleep. Every day after that, he continued to watch her, as she concentrated in class, as she talked to her schoolmates, as she sat in the evenings under the trees, and read.

She had encountered his gaze one day, and a warm glow had spread inside of her, something that she tucked away in a safe place, like a treasure in a chest, to be opened when she chose. Occasionally she would look up and meet his eyes and when she did, each of them would feel an electric current run through their bodies, a current that was mild at first, and startled each of them. They would look down as shyness overtook them.

They began talking for hours, under that tree, day after day, about books, about philosophy, about poetry, about love. While their tastes were different, they learned from each other, as they shared their passions, their stories, other people's stories, the history of the world. They both loved the ocean, and the sea for them reigned in its majesty, and called out to them as individuals, as a pair. They loved the foam from the water as it mixed with the salt in the air, creating a space of endless possibilities. And, after discussing and sharing, they would find each other's lips and find places of passion in them they never knew existed.

And under that mulberry tree, the day after Talia's birthday, this man knelt and held Talia's soft hand, asking for her permission to be his bride. Love blended with humility and joy on his face that was met with a simple "Yes", as the breeze caressed her face, eyes, tearing up, such beauty in her love for him, in his love for her, those two children growing up in a time of war, yet finding their own paradise amidst it.

I looked at Ishmael and saw tears coming from his face. Such tenderness from this young man, whose story moved him as much as me. He put his hand to his heart, as he paused, took a deep breath, and smiled at his own victories, at his own dreams that had come true. Love spread across his face, the antidote to all the pain he had experienced from his youth. He was a man now, and that was clear in his story and in the ensuing ending that he was giving to me on that night before his wedding.

And so, he concluded, two months after this young man would propose to his beloved Talia, the castle would close its doors, and the children would find homes elsewhere: in England, in Scotland and Ireland, in Palestine, in America, in Australia, in France. Everything had been arranged, and the cartons and valises were opened as a mad frenzy occurred to fill them. Everyone prepared for the grand departure from the haven of Clonyn Castle. But before the children dispersed themselves to their new destinations, everyone piled on several buses that departed to the west of the country, to County Kerry, home to writers and artists, and painters, and above all, the sea.

The small town of Ballybunion welcomed them all with abundance. The generosity of the Irish people and the land bathed them with life and an everlasting love, as colors and beginnings surrounded them.

He was silent, then, my storyteller, this beautiful man who had

survived, found love, ready to begin his life with another. We each took
our glasses and made a toast to love, to this survival, to the story that
tells it.

The next day, as I sat on that hillside, I watched, one by one, the
entire town arrive at the wedding. Everyone brought flowers and food
and loving gestures. I watched one hundred children get off buses
and join all the children and all the adults of my town. I watched all
these people circle around Talia and Ishmael, laughing and dancing,
celebrating the union of these two beautiful beings. Their limbs were
loose and free, and a dazzling light filled their faces, a luminescence
as bright as a glorious full moon.

Yes, new beginnings surrounded them all, in this portrait of one
hundred children, embraced and held by a nation, bathed in life, forty
shades of it.

RAPPROCHEMENT

The first time I saw her she was eating yogurt in the snow. Her matted dark hair enveloped her long face. It was the first day of winter in Paris. I had woken up that morning and looked out the window to witness the first dancing flakes that were swirling effortlessly through the sky. Their silence hushed the intensity of the city. I had left my apartment that day like a child who forgets each year what snow is about, mesmerized once again by its delicate softness, by ice itself falling from a gray limitless sky, by its whiteness, so white it dazzles the mind during this time of darkness and introspection.

I walked around my neighborhood, entranced by the jewels created by ice. I had ended up around the corner at the grayed seventeenth century Gothic church, laced with white, dark spires that reached towards the sky. There she was, with no shoes on, huddling in the bushes on top of the new snow. She was eating yogurt from a small container.

I couldn't help but stare. I, the psychologist and writer, spy of other peoples' intriguing lives, couldn't help but fix my eyes on this striking woman eating yogurt on the first day of winter while Paris moved around her in amorphous ways.

She looked up, saw my glazing intrusive eyes, and she gave me a look of disdain, reminding me that I am I and she is she, and borders and limits are to be respected. Yet, was it my imagination, or did it really happen, a tiny glimpse of need that slipped out of the protective barriers of the human species, a subtle glance from her eyes to mine that seeped out in a miniscule trickle, that spelled: *help me; I am alone, and please help.*

I knew better than approaching her, even to smile at her. But my curiosity took over, and she was all I thought about for the next few days.

I returned towards the church. This time, though, I went across the street and sat at a café, pretending to write on my laptop. It had snowed again the night before, and the frigid morning temperatures were giving way to a crystal-clear day.

As I was slowly sipping my tea, I saw her again out of the corner of my eye. She appeared to be circling the church, walking around and around its outside perimeter. Occasionally she would look up into the tree that bordered the small garden. From my vantage point, it seemed as if this tree had some grounding force for her. Each time she would make this circle and look up into this tree, barren of leaves, she would smile, being met perhaps in the simple glance at a wintered horse chestnut, its limbs like small fists, knotty and solid. Noon approached and the bell chimed, as do so many church bells in France. From across the street where I was sitting, a woman approached with a plastic shopping bag that dangled from her arm. Looking away, careful to not as much as glance at the woman who had stopped for a moment her church circling, this woman put the plastic bag down on the ground by the bushes. Then she left, disappearing into the momentum of the city that surrounded us all.

The woman I sat staring at seemed used to this routine and this other woman who brought her food. Nonchalantly she opened the bag. She took out a sandwich that was carefully wrapped up in paper. In my mind, I wished her *bon appétit,* a blessing over the meal, while she looked up into the sky and touched the sandwich. She took a bite and then another; afterwards she pulled out an apple, and a dessert, something that resembled a cake. She seemed content. The world fed her. What is it in a person, I wondered, who does not have a home, or appears not to have one that connects them to the world, that allows them a sense of place?

After the meal, she sat quietly huddled again in the bushes, no longer involved in the anxious circling behavior of the morning. From the plastic bag, she dragged out something else, a magazine, and for the next hour or so, she stared intensely at each page. She seemed to find something that completely engrossed her that created an infinite solitary intimate space.

I left her ensconced in the magazine. I was piqued by what exactly she was looking at, but I knew I would have to wait to find more clues. I made my way up the circuitous staircase of my home, a studio flat in the heart of the Marais, where I was surrounded by the clicks of heels and the aromas of freshly baked pita bread and strudel every day.

This was my year to thrive in Paris and to write, I had told myself. I had bumbled through a messy divorce, bitterness still on my tongue as I had slipped onto the ferry, one suitcase in hand, from the island in the Pacific Northwest I was living in, to Paris. In my mind, I believed this destination would give me perspective and a treasured escape from the insidiousness of the breakup of what was once my entire life, to the next passage of my existence that felt entirely nebulous. My ex-husband and I had no children, as we had devoted our entire married lives to our work, partnering in our psychology practice in downtown Seattle.

A year ago, when he had announced he was having an affair, it was one of those days where hidden beauty was what one had to keep inside. In between clients, I had watched from my window a steady rain, water that flowed effortlessly from the sky. I had not wanted to take the ferry that day to our home, our secluded lush abode overlooking the Puget Sound, a protected fantasy existence that I thought would never end. He, the psychologist, had refused couples' therapy, as he wore a silver engagement ring on the hand that used to hold our marriage's one in gold.

I had cried in between clients for that entire year, sleeping on friends' couches, not wanting to smell his sweet aroma that had now turned bitter in what was to be our forever home. After a year of this, after we were officially divorced, I decided, one sleepless night, when aches all over my body had taken control and made me feel like I would be eternally disabled, that I would take a sabbatical and leave the Northwest and move to Paris, a place that had always been an important part of my life.

As I made my way to the top of the staircase in my year's sublet on the rue Vieille du Temple, I put my one-hundred-year-old-key into the lock, letting the smells of Paris filter through me like a warm balm. I sighed as I was entering my apartment, letting go of the hellacious year I had just experienced into the mysterious haze of what was lying right in front of me.

* * *

The day's impressions swam in my head: a so far unnamed woman with olive skin and an unmistakable rich history. I was allured by her simplicity, her depth, and her story.

For the next few days, I distractedly worked on my book—ironically on the topic of rapprochement. My research was based on the work of the renowned psychologist Margaret Mahler, that focused on the moments when a very young child leaves their own world, and seeks out a vital relationship with their mother, the all too vital beginnings of the sense of self and other. For years, I had been looking at this issue on many levels in my work, with children, adults and communities, examining how rapprochement was vital in its ways of creating peace in a world that was fraught with so much disconnect among people.

Rapprochement. I was steeped in material observing the unnamed woman on the church grounds in the 3rd *arrondissement* in Paris. While I was writing, I suddenly realized my observations the other day had led me to crave a rapprochement with her. I thought about how I might make this connection, one that would forge a gap between us. I wondered if our common ground could be loneliness.

The next day, I omitted my laptop in my bag and instead stuffed it with pens, paints and pencils of all kinds and colors, canvases, a fold up easel and a folding chair, having gone crazy in the BHV's art department. There she was, sitting in the bushes, peering at the same magazine as the last time I saw her. Without looking at her, I found an inconspicuous spot to sit, setting up my makeshift art studio. I stood far enough away to give her space, yet close enough to pique her curiosity. Using my rudimentary art skills from my high school days, I focused on the tree, the one she seemed to revere, and began to sketch, noticing how I felt absorbed in this activity, losing all sense of other, as I engaged in my art and the space of my own imagination. Yet my third eye noticed that she came closer to me to observe what I was doing. I wanted to meet her eyes so badly, to begin that contact that I craved with her, yet I also knew, from all my research, that rapprochement is a subtle process, one that takes patience and time.

Day after day for two weeks I did this each morning. I absorbed myself in my drawing of the tree, capturing all its nuances and shadings. Each day she edged closer. By the end of the second week, she ended

up right next to my canvas, and she pointed to the part I was drawing. She shook her head and then looked up into the tree and showed
me how I had missed one of the crevices that formed the branches.
I looked up too, then down at my drawing, and giggled, acknowledging that she was spot on. A faint turn of her lips indicated that she
agreed, and she laughed. In my heart, I could have hugged her. In my
actions, I smiled, putting away my canvas for the day, remembering my
grandmother's words of wisdom: always to leave the table a bit hungry.

I waited a few days before going back, wanting to let that monumental accomplishment between us sit and settle. On Monday of the
following week I returned, this time with a burning desire to finish
the tree. I set up my canvas, and as I was getting ready to start, she approached me, her magazine tucked under her arm. She sat on the grass.
I sat down next to her, holding my breath. She opened a page and then
pointed to a picture. It showed a woman in a place that seemed rather
other worldly, making yogurt in the snow. She stopped at this page and
smiled, truly, transported to a distant dream, yet one that beckoned her
with every breath. She flipped to the cover of the magazine, letting me
see the title: *Iceland.* I shivered inside, not from the cold and the images
of snow and ice, but just from the name itself which evoked mystery
and an other- worldliness, a land so far away, yet not.

As she stared at page after page of her magazine, I, too, felt a pull
inside me to visit this country, to witness the starkness of the landscape. She landed again on the picture of the woman making yogurt
in the snow, and together, we smiled as we observed the face of the
yogurt maker, surrounded by ice and an absence of vegetation. There
was something there, a depth, that one could not ignore. We both nodded and smiled. In that nod, we silently understood that we were both
allured by this image and this country. Our shared experience was

our secret, a feeling of intimacy that moved beyond the pages of this tourist magazine.

That night I had a dream: I was flying on a plane, and it landed in the middle of a hill of ice, yet all around this hill there were green fields and poppies growing.

On impulse, I went to the travel agency later that morning and bought two airline tickets-Paris to Reykjavik. Less than a month later, I would be sitting on a plane heading towards the land of ice and yogurt, next to an unnamed woman with a language and a history I still had no knowledge of. Yet, she had a charm that directed itself into my heart with inspiration alone.

I felt completely insane, yet insanely happy.

The next day I was in the grocery store, perusing the isles of coffee, and a man approached me. From his dress, I could tell he was a priest.

"*Excusez-moi* Madame," he started. "I am the priest of *l'église Mariavite* on the *rue Aubriot*. I have wanted to talk to you about the woman you have been observing and spending time with over the past few weeks, but I never wanted to disturb. I am so glad to see you now."

I asked about the woman, explained my situation, stating that there were so many intriguing mysteries about her.

He nodded in agreement. "Ah, how I wish I could tell you her story, but all I know is that she is a refugee from Syria. She arrived alone in Paris six months ago and was directed to a shelter but refused to stay there. She does not speak any French, and when she was approached in Arabic, she seemed to understand but did not answer. So, we have no information about her. She ended up at our church and I took her in. She sleeps on a bed we made up for her in the basement, and once a day, one of the women of the church comes and brings her food. My impression of her is that she has had a traumatic experience, on top of being a refugee escaping the violence and the injustices that have been perpetuated from the Syrian crisis. But she seems safe here at the church, and with you, which is comforting to all of us."

I nodded and shared my observations with him, particularly her fascination for Iceland. I suggested I take her there for a while, letting her have an experience that she seems hungry for. His eyes lit up when I suggested it; I could clearly see that he cared.

The next day I enrolled in a weekend intensive Arabic language course. For thirty hours, three solid days, ten hours a day, I was immersed in the sounds and textures of a language that was so different from French and English—the only two languages I knew. The first two days I listened. As I observed and absorbed, I sunk into the world of this language. Already, by the second night, I began to have dreams in Arabic, and the softness and the hardness of its sounds swam through my unconscious mind. By the third and final day I began to speak roughly but at the end of the day, I felt my tongue wrapped around the vowels and consonants, as I folded myself around a language that represented a non-Western culture, one so different from my own. Yet, I believe we all have a language in the world that represents the part of us that never gets expressed, and I know for certain that Arabic was that language for me. The more I listened to it, the more I felt something opening inside of me, a cave unexplored, waiting, resonating with a passion that I needed to discover.

I realized I was uncovering my own need for rapprochement with myself, through a language that would reveal not only discreet aspects of who I was, but of so many people speaking it every single day. I longed to enter the space of Arabic, hearing it in all forms. As we left the class, the teachers gave all the students a stack of flyers and announcements for Arabic cultural events and places to visit in Paris. I specifically asked about Syrian gatherings.

Quietly, the next morning I approached the unnamed woman. When she saw me, she smiled wide, her mouth forming a lovely shape, inviting me in. In Arabic, I spoke:

"My name is Jasmine."

"Ah, Yasmin!" she said, seemingly stunned I had spoken her language.

"What is yours?" I said slowly, trying to wrap those few Arabic words around my tongue, letting them effortlessly flow out with a rhythm in the voice, a song.

"Mine is Yesinia. Also, a flower, she said in Arabic." Again, she smiled, sweetness covering her face, the simple recognition between us that we were both born of flowers, beauty from different sides of the world.

"Yesinia." I repeated, loving the way it rolled off my tongue. "That is a beautiful name."

She blushed and looked down. "Yes. As is yours. Where did you learn Arabic?"

I told her and then I showed her the pamphlets, the huge stack that fell from my hands.

Her face suddenly changed. Gone was the easy comfort in her expression, the trust, the smile, and instead, fear seemed to blanket her being as she closed her eyes.

"I am sorry." I whispered. "I am sorry."

She walked to the bushes and sat down on the grass, motioning me with her eyes to sit next to her quietly. I folded my legs, and for the next few hours we sat together, not uttering a word. I wondered what caused her panic and then saw clearly how trauma surrounded her past. I wept inside for this agony she experienced. The woman came at noon, with the plastic bag. I saw she was hungry, ravenous, as she blessed its contents, looking up at the sky and touching the paper that held the sandwich. She motioned for me to share, but I did not dare take away her precious meal, ending with a container of yogurt.

"Yogurt," I said, breaking our silence.

"Yes," she answered quietly.

"Yogurt in Iceland," I added.

"Yes!" She looked in my eyes, her smile returning, the tiny folds of skin curving up to the sky, her mind appearing to relax.

When she finished her meal, I reached into my handbag and brought out the airline tickets. My hands shook; my heart was not sure if it was the right time, especially after her experience earlier.

Her eyes looked inquisitively at the writing in front of her.

"Airline tickets. You and me. To Iceland," I said slowly and carefully in Arabic, glancing at her face. I didn't want to miss something.

She pointed to me. Then to herself, her eyes showing a question.

"Yes," I replied.

She sat there, in the bushes, her feet wrapped around each other, looked down, and then she looked up into the tree, whose limbs had begun to show tiny buds. She looked down again and closed her eyes for maybe two minutes. I watched her and waited.

When she opened her eyes and gazed in mine, I saw sweetness and excitement there, like a flower opening itself up after several months of hiding. She said quietly in her native language: "Yes. You and me. In Iceland."

I smiled and looked back into the spark in her eyes, beaming from mine to hers.

"When?" She added.

"Next week."

We sat side by side. Knowing that we would depart soon could only connect us deeper, into the space shared by two people looking forward to doing something together.

We giggled like two schoolgirls as the day moved around us. We took in the movement of Paris that we heard, but only what we cared to, as we sat together, quietly chuckling, our smiles passing from one to the other. She held the tickets in her hand, stroking them.

As the afternoon turned to early evening, I got up to go. She handed me back the tickets and I carefully put them in my handbag as I said goodbye and moved into the crowd. I felt light and happy on my way home, climbing the spiral staircase and entering the welcoming scents of the world that was mine, now embellished by another in my heart.

The next night I headed to the Métro, to a destination that was written on one of the flyers. As the train moved from stop to stop, I noted the changes in the people who got on and off. By the time we reached my stop, in the 13th arrondissement, the metro stop Place d'Italie, I noticed I was the only white person getting off the train. Walking through the streets, I sensed I was stared at.

Once at the restaurant, I lost track of time as I sat at a table and my mind drifted to Yesinia. I had a picture in my mind now of her beautiful face lit up by her smile, saying her name, as she let the idea of going to Iceland with me filter in, bit by bit. I sensed that, in doing this, she was letting go of something monumental in her life that had traumatized her greatly. The secret of the yogurt was still mine to figure out, yet I had an intuitive feeling that there was something about this food that brought her back to her roots.

A few days later, I stepped out of the taxi, my suitcase in the trunk and the two airline tickets in my bag. I stood in front of the church and gasped as I witnessed construction workers putting up a metal fence around the church. I could not see Yesinia in her usual spot, which was now barricaded.

I stormed up to one of the workers, demanding to know what was going on. He said they had been contracted to paint and put in a new plumbing system, and the church grounds had been blocked off for safety.

"Have you seen a dark-haired woman, dark skin, anywhere around?" My voice was high pitched, and extremely anxious.

"No Madame but ask that man over there. He's our boss."

I went over to the man who appeared to be the boss—big and rather threatening in his body posturing. He told me the woman was in the church, waiting for me.

I rushed in, panting with relief, and there she was, sitting quietly, staring at the stain glass windows, her hands in her lap. Her face looked shaken, but calm. Her shoulder-length hair was washed and shone in the dim light of the church. Her clothes were clean, and her dark boots looked almost new. She held around her arm a leather handbag, and from her ears dangled gold earrings, matching the many gold bracelets she was wearing. She was gorgeous, transformed, and seemingly ready to move into the next phase of her life.

"Are we ready to go?" she asked.

"Yes, the taxi is waiting."

We slipped into the back seats and watched Paris move its delicate fibers around us as we gazed out the window, making our way to Charles de Gaulle Airport.

The cacophony of the airport excited us, knowing that we were leaving it. All at once I began to panic, thinking that Yesinia had no passport, as a refugee. We were next in line, and the customs officer looked me up and down, which made me suspicious of his intentions.

He asked her for identification, and from her handbag, she produced a passport. I glanced over at it. It was to expire in two months. "Refugee" was stamped on it. I looked over at her as we passed through security and as we put things in plastic tubs. She had nothing.

Finally, Iceland Air was ready for us, and we sat in our seats. We took off, and the plane lifted higher, flying into the depths of clouds and turbulent air. I felt Yesinia relax next to me, her breath slow and even, and when I looked over at her, she sighed. I sighed myself, feeling a similar transformative energy inside me. It did not seem long before our ears began popping, announcing a descent into a different world. I watched out of the window at ice infused with sheer rock, grays and lustering browns. Starkness enveloped us.

Snow met us as we got off the plane and exited the terminal, white and grey. A cold wind blew at our necks. We each stretched out our tongues, like children, tasting the freshness of Icelandic snow. We laughed.

Instantly we seemed to have fallen in love with this country.

I found the rental car I had reserved, and for several days I drove us to places that seemed untouched, stopping almost every two seconds to photograph the majesty of this land. I stopped occasionally, talking to people, marveling at the sincere kindness and generosity of each one. We ate in restaurants, delighted in the new tastes that continually warmed our bellies. We sat quietly and listened to the sounds of silence in this quiet, respectful land of the natural world. We swam in the Blue Lagoon, and felt like queens in a primeval mysterious land, generations ago, bathed by water that heals and calms the senses.

We looked at art, all kinds of it, and walked away speechless by the massive creativity that inhabited this land of mystery. We found ourselves mesmerized by the ponies, wild and full of their own magic of this land. We picked up volcanic rocks, feeling their energy, the presence of volcanic activity everywhere, this nation of earthly turbulence, yet so unspoiled in its pure state of grace. Iceland had entered our pores, our very being in the most sensual and tantalizing ways a land can enter a person.

At one point, Yesinia looked at me and simply said: "Yogurt."

She said this as I was driving, deep in thought and captivated by the world around me.

As if there was something in her head that read what was not there, at that moment a sign appeared, a local farm. I swerved, taking the small dirt road to the very end. The snow had barely started to melt here, and the wind was blowing around the bend when we arrived at a small house.

We knocked on the door, and I soon realized my English and French and her Arabic would get us nowhere. I went back to the car and found a container of yogurt, which we held up to the woman who answered the door. There was a harshness in her face that mimicked the landscape, yet also a depth of experience, a kindness in her movements, in her speech, even if we knew not a word she was saying. She motioned for us to follow, and we did. She showed us where she made her yogurt and demonstrated to us how she did it. Yesinia looked at the woman and nodded, showing in her face that she knew exactly what she was talking about. They each pointed and used their hands, expressing what their common ground was, their shared passion. All at once I understood, and I knew, the picture of Yesinia's life, the story that created who she was, and the reason she was here. The woman found a calendar and pointed to the day we were on, and pointed to two days later, a Monday, and she pointed to Yesinia, that she could come there and make yogurt.

I witnessed all this pointing and felt tears well up inside of me, seeing home written on her face, her face that had witnessed so much.

That night, in the house I had rented for the two of us, we made a fire and sat outside. It was clear and sharp. The moon and stars emerged from the sky like a piece of theatre. Looking up, we saw flashes of color everywhere, the Northern Lights giving us a celebration of all that was and had been.

Yesinia took my hand and held it as I sighed, loving the softness of her skin on mine.

As we slept that night, we folded our bodies around each other. Millions of colored lights in the sky surrounded us.

* * *

Yesinia began making yogurt, and I phoned my ex-husband, telling him I would not be coming back to Seattle. The practice was his now. All my clients, anyway, had departed before I left, as we carefully planned. Each one I had helped to find their own source of love and nourishment. In one week, the realtor sold the house. Freedom felt so tangible at that moment.

Yet the true freedom was right in front of me, waking up every morning and kissing Yesinia's face, the woman that was my life, a million secret stars in blazing colors.

She taught me Arabic, and I taught her English, and as our skills at communicating improved, our conversations took on a language of stories, becoming more and more detailed with time.

Little by little she shared with me everything about her life before she met me, up until the day her husband and her daughter died on the boat coming here in Europe, diseased throughout their bodies, as she wailed helplessly, and the waves incessantly crashed all around them. She told me of her farm in Syria, before the war, and that her yogurt was prized throughout the region, its texture and taste only for the gods, her customers had said. She told me of a life that unraveled bit by bit, as their lives became not their own anymore, and they had to escape to survive. She told me more, and often at the end of each story, she would then take my hand, which became a signal to me that she needed quiet, a space to breathe, a different reality.

We bought a house, one that would allow her to make her own yogurt, and I to continue writing. We found a home that signaled the forever quality in our relationship. It was a beautiful house that over-looked the mountains and the water, that had a farm and everything she needed to make the best yogurt in the region, as the locals all said. My book, finished, became indeed a bestseller. And as that work ended, more ideas continued to filter through me. I embraced an infinite de-sire to keep writing. Yesinia, becoming more proficient now in English, became my editor, my muse, my guide in all things. I knew she loved to read my writing, and I loved to sit by the fire and read her aloud what had transpired from my brain to the paper. Day by day we grew old together, although we did not see it as age, but more so, a coming together of two people, irrespective of language and culture and time itself. What we had together was transcendence, a forging of a quiet space that was limitless in its possibilities, that spoke of the heart and its regular beat, a movement in the ephemeral world of love and its endless range of motion.

SEIZURE

Her entire life, or at least that which she was conscious of, changed that day in the operating theatre. Images flashed before her eyes: her three children, hugging her goodbye before the school bus whisked them away, rambling over country roads, as the sheep bayed and the rain poured down. In their bags that day she had put little notes, one for each of them, telling them how much she loved them. Once a week or so Laurel did this, smiling, as she would carefully fold each piece of paper, imagining the happy look on her daughters' faces upon finding them. Every now and then they would let on they had received those little notes. She knew, as mothers do, how much they loved those words, those reminders from home when they were at school and home seemed very far away.

After they had left for school that morning and their laughter had long silenced in her small house, everything began. It was her day off.

The nausea came first that had gripped her like a noose, then the pangs in her abdomen, fierce balls of fire that had erupted in her body. She grabbed the table; vomit spewed everywhere. The pain increased, far worse than childbirth—the three times in her life where she had experienced torrential pain. No, this was worse, she decided, as she tried to pick up her cell phone, but her arm hit it, and she watched it drop to the floor. She became delirious, her mind like glue as the throbbing violence inside her body incessantly wavered between ten and twenty. She nearly passed out, and her head barely missed the table leg, as her body fell to the floor. She was a tangled mass of pain sprawled out in her own sickness.

Somehow, she managed to grab the phone and called ooo. The operator in Melbourne answered right away. She could not speak through the knives that ceaselessly stabbed her insides, and after several attempts, she gave up and let the phone sit idly by her side. A half hour passed, maybe longer. She tried again. Her fingers managed to press ooo. Again, an operator answered. Again, she could not say a word. The operator tried to ask her questions over and over. She couldn't hear anything she said, the pain's voice was so loud. Finally, with a burst of tears her voice screamed out: "775 Burgess Street. Pain."

An hour later she was in the operating theatre. Dimmed lights floated in and out as she was lying on the table. She had gone unconscious in the ambulance, and when she had arrived in the emergencies room, she regained consciousness, as bursts of pain invaded her body.

The anesthesiologist walked in and spoke to her as the nurses were preparing her for surgery.

"What drug will you be using, Doctor?" she managed to ask, her survival instincts kicking in. Her twenty-five years as an RN allowed her a good deal of knowledge regarding pharmaceuticals, and for the briefest moment her brain slipped away from the pain and moved it aside, the warrior inside of her needed to know.

"Flexidone," he answered flatly, seemingly annoyed with her question. "Now, just relax. You have a severe case of appendicitis. We need to proceed. I am a busy man."

"NO!", Laurel screamed. "This is a dangerous drug. It has been known to cause severe seizures." Somewhere, buried in the agony that plagued every one of her cells, she recalled several articles she had read about this dangerous drug that was new and cheap—insurance companies were vying for it.

"I am the doctor, and I decide these things. Unless you have a known allergy, I will be using this drug. You will be fine. Just relax. We need to move quickly before the infection goes into your brain."

"NO. PLEASE, Doctor. Find something else!"

After that, everything happened very quickly. The curtain closed around her, and the nurses gave her the injection into her IV. Slowly the drug moved from the needle into her vein and her brain quieted, as she was lying motionless.

Three hours later in the recovery room, it had all gone dark, and the nightmare began. First the wheezing, then the convulsing, then the thrashing. The attending doctor was immediately called in. He had never seen a grand mal seizure as demonic as this one.

Later that day, there was another.

And again, the next day, just as severe.

Then, they stopped, and Laurel was released from the hospital. They said the operation had been successful, focusing on just that. The doctor tried to convince her the seizures were a freak thing, a psychosomatic response to surgery, and that they would go away. Laurel knew better.

The seizures never stopped. Every single day, her body became a wreck. She never knew when they would arrive, the maimed visitor at the door who would storm in and take her body and her soul away for minutes, hours—she never knew how long. No medications seemed to work, as still the demon persisted, screaming in her ear, sending a tempest through her brain.

She had long since quit her job, so she sat at home every day, awaiting disaster. Her life had become expectant of it.

Her children seemed to be afraid of her. The youngest one begged her to come back to her. She held her baby, just five years old, and cried. She remembered the day she was born, and the light shining through the windows, fluttering the lace curtains. There had been such a violent storm that day that she had been unable to get to the hospital and her best friend had had to deliver the baby at home, in her bed. The moment she had emerged from her womb, the rain stopped, and the sun appeared, like a jewel out of the mud. She had named her Soleil, the sun.

Her husband had convinced her children that she had gone insane. One night, when she was asleep, he left with them, and they all went to his parents' house. He had told the police to put out a restraining order and managed to convince them that she was no longer a fit parent.

Laurel woke up the next morning to find an empty house. She phoned everywhere and then discovered everything. She saw her life; she saw it, bleeding through the cracks in the walls. As her body convulsed, thrashing wildly, tearing down the curtains that waved once so gently, just five years ago. She screamed, feeling her rage at the doctor who had not cared to listen.

She knew she needed help. Again, she called ooo. She was not sure if this was a bad or a good decision, but she felt desperate.

The paramedics took her to the hospital, where she stayed for two months. Finally, at the end of this time, the seizures calmed, and as she walked up her driveway, she smelled something quite odd, not the familiar scents of home. She went to her front door, and the key did not work. She peered in the windows and saw furniture that was not her own.

She went to the next-door neighbor's house and knocked on the door. An older woman let her in.

"What happened?" came out of her mouth.

The neighbor sighed. "Your husband has a new wife. A month ago, a moving truck came and took everything. I don't know where they moved to."

Laurel gulped. "And the children?"

"They are all together."

She gripped the table.

"Laurel, honey. There is a restraining order. And, oh, this is for you." She handed her a thick envelope. Laurel ripped it open: divorce papers.

Laurel stepped out of the house and began to walk. She walked for miles, over hills, through gullies, across farms, the tears wedged inside of her, the screams latently waiting for something hiding behind polished stones in that marred landscape that was now her life.

She wanted to howl but couldn't. She wanted to fight but the weapons inside of her felt dark, limp. She wanted to grab her children and run away, but her arms felt useless. She wanted to remember what she felt, the day she had gotten married to the prince of her dreams, how happy she was. But all that came to her memories was an obscured photograph, damaged by the rain, the damp, a sickening mold covering all.

The ensuing weeks, months, years blurred together in a maze that tangled around her brain. The seizures, only twice a week or so now, allowed her a moment's respite. In those lucid moments, she tried to sue the hospital, but the statute of limitations had expired. She tried to regain custody of her children or at least to have contact with them. She wanted to tell them she loved them. Each time she pleaded, each time her heart pumped wildly, and she got shoved even further in the darkened corner. She was blocked from all social media, from phone contact, and from finding out where her children were. While she was in the hospital her father had died, and her mother, who had adored her ex-husband, had not communicated once with Laurel.

One day, she arrived at her mother's front door. Blithely, the woman who had not birthed her but had signed papers proving guardianship, said: "Oh, but I would have helped you, if only you had asked."

"Where are my children?"

"They are with their father and his new wife, somewhere in America. First, they said they would be in New York, and then they said Chicago, but I am not sure at all if they got there. I just can't keep track of them," she laughed.

Laurel seethed inside. She looked in her eyes, tasting the bitterness of deceit, the lies unfurled, the deception shimmying around this woman who stood facing her at the door, not even letting her in.

It rained hard that day. Laurel walked away, into the pounding jets of water that immersed themselves in her body. Her tears finally emerged and mingled with the rain and the darkness that encompassed a life, her life. She fell to the earth, and the mud caked on all sides of her, as she groveled in it like a boar, still crying. She cried because of the injustice of it all, breeding itself on the weak, on the wounded, the sick and the small person who just wanted to live. She bawled, as she remembered her babies, each one of them, their tininess enfolded around her, her breasts, their nourishment, their lives exploding as their soft infant lips suckled. She felt her barrenness, naked in that sodden dirt. Her hands grasped at the air, those lives that came from her, now gone, away, her life obliterated from theirs. She screamed. She wanted them back; she wanted her life back; she wanted a life.

She felt hungry, ravished.

Later, she returned to her tiny shack of a home, sat in the bath, and let the warmth filter through her, as the water rinsed off the dirt. She felt a tiny window open as she dried off and collapsed on her bed into a deep sleep, wrapped up in layers upon layers of blankets. Somewhere in her dreams that night, she thought she found home.

The next day she phoned her only friend, Indira. They had been friends since the birth of their children, and she was the one person who had not run away from her.

"Come over," she said.

She was in the kitchen cooking. Laurel watched, saying nothing, recording in her mind the spices her friend poured in, the amounts of chickpeas and lentils and rice and the ways they were blended and cooked.

"Everything I make," she said, "I learned from my family in Bombay."

At lunch, together at the table, Laurel melted into the aromas that were on her palate, each bite like a blessing to her wounded soul. When she left her friend's house, she felt her steps lighter, so light she could have danced home.

After that day, Laurel began to cook. Spices flooded her senses, her dreams, and her visions. She concocted, mixed, poured, baked and cooked over her small stove. As she fed herself, bite by bite, she noticed her seizures begin to diminish. Her energy returned, and in her broken mirror in the bathroom she smiled, staring at herself for the first time in years.

She created a blog, wanting to share her recipes with anyone who would care to listen to and read her creations, her story. She wanted to reach out her hand and feel others reaching for it, a small grasp in the space of the immensity around her.

And then one day it happened. One restaurant, two, more, contacted her, wanting her recipes, wanting her to be their guest chef.

She looked radiant that day, stepping out of her home, her cheeks flushed, reminding her of the moment she had found out she was pregnant for the first time. She walked into the restaurant, glowing, rolled up her sleeves: the huge kitchen awaited her, its bowls and pots glimmering from the sunlight that poured into the windows. Focused on each of the spices, each morsel of food that she blended with them, she created. Her art became the nourishment of souls that day, that day that lasted lifetimes, hers and so many more, in that kitchen, in lives that needed a soul, all the damaged wings coming home to rest.

JOURNEYS

The sound of drums echoed over the Puget Sound, to Seattle and back. The sun started to emerge, tantalizing rays that beamed through clouds as scattered raindrops fell playfully through the sky. The women swayed on the beach, shaking rattles, while drums beat and voices chanted, welcoming the canoe, the first of many.

The crowd cheered and the rhythm of the carved oars kept its pace: sixteen oars, eight pullers. They appeared tired, yet seemed buoyed by the drums, their people waiting for them, the land. This was the end of their third day of the tribal journey, and the first canoe had just come in. It began two days earlier, at the southern end of Washington State. They had said that visions directed them to their destination: the northern region of BC, Powell River. They would meet up with dozens of tribes from the Pacific Northwest.

But while the drums continued the meditative rhythms, and they pulled each stroke, each movement of the water into the taut muscles of their arms, their focus was clearly on the present. They made a circle at the beach, while the applause resonated from the shore. Then they came to a stop, and in unison, they raised their oars to the vertical, aligning sky and land.

"We are the Nisaguamish tribe!" a puller announced, standing up in the canoe. Pride filled her voice. She gripped her oar like a talisman while she stood. Her long dark hair floated around her face, the flickering sun illuminating her smile.

Lynette stared from the canoe ramp and teared up. *She is still as beautiful as ever.*

The applause was thick, heavy with sound, when the pullers emerged from their canoes, one by one. Lynette tried to stifle her memories as her hands came together and clapped. Everything hurt. Her body was now a mass of crippled thorns.

Sylvane walked up the ramp, her hands empty, beaming quietly to herself. Lynette tried to catch her eye. Sylvane looked up and she gazed for a split second at Lynette. Nodding, her face flushed, she continued with the others. Lynette followed her with her eyes. She looked down at her muscled calves, remembering her softness. So many years later, she had never stopped missing her.

Canoe after canoe came in after that first one, each one from a different tribe. The rhythm of the drums was like meditation, the chanting and the rattling accompanied the applause.

This was her home; finally, she had found it. After so many years searching, being denied home, her culture, her place, Lynette—or Ette, as everyone called her—had landed on the banks of this place, the tribe that had always been hers. Once she arrived, she knew she would never leave. On her head was a cap of woven cedar; around her were forests of cedars, the ones she hugged when the pain got too bad. Every day she wore her favorite jacket, the tattered leather a soft contrast to all the inscriptions and patches on it, reminding her of her life, the wounded vet she had become.

She smelled the fires around her, the cedar smoke of home, of ritual, dinner being cooked.

She wanted to forget.

Everyone knew her. She was the one who gave hugs, who had smiles for everyone, who ran the food bank in town for all the locals, for her people who were so often hungry. She knew the ones who wouldn't take enough, and she would always slip in an extra loaf of bread, a bag of fruit. She knew the ones who would take too much, filling their woven baskets with an abundance, way more than they needed. She would wink at them, reminding them that next time, try to go a bit easy when it was their turn.

While the canoes circled around the beach, awaiting their turn for their welcome to Quilomish land, Ette's thoughts turned to Sylvane's hair, how it glistened just moments before, memories of it lodged now in her brain. Hours and hours were spent stroking it, their skin naked, strands wrapped around her like lace.

Her body began to shiver, and her breath became shallow. She began to sweat uncontrollably, and her heart rate increased. She knew all these PTSD symptoms. She hated them. One of her aunties, spotting her, came to her quickly and put her arm around her. Her laughter swallowed her up. She could begin to breathe again from the embrace.

"Hiya, Ette. A lot more youth this year!" she said quietly, trying to get her niece's mind off what was getting at it.

"Yeah, did you hear that kid? He said to his uncle, 'I fell asleep three times!'"

"Just like my grand baby. The rhythm of the oars, the water and sun put him to sleep, too."

The two women stood side by side and looked around. They each knew that family puts everything back together again. The drumbeats continued; the droplets of rain had long since stopped.

*　*　*

Ette, alone again and feeling a little more stable, made her way through the crowd, where all the canoes lay resting. Everyone had come in, and the carved-out cedar trees sat quietly. Each one had a story; each sacred tribal journey was imprinted in the wood. She put her hand on one, feeling its smoothness under her fingertips. Without even looking, her hand grazed the sides of the canoe that Sylvane had been in, that had belonged for generations to the Nisaguamish tribe.

She looked up, feeling her presence near, her energy like a magnet. From the corners of her eyes, she saw her standing and talking, laughing with the other pullers. She looked tired and sore. Ette wanted to put her arms around her, to feel her sinking again into them. She was known throughout the community as a tribal healer, the one who could pull pain. With Sylvane, all she had to do was to hold her for two seconds, and immediately she felt everything begin to release. Ette's hands would do all the work while Sylvane would breathe into the folds of her, listening to her moan, pain escaping from her body.

Ette moved away from the canoes and walked over to the food table where there was a huge canister of water. She took a cup, filled it and let the cool fluid sink into her parched insides. No matter what kind of weather the Pacific Northwest was graced with, she was always hot. She chatted with the women who were setting up the tables. Everyone was family to her and her to them. There wasn't much they didn't know about her. Secrets were for white people, they always said, laughing.

The smoke from the salmon cooking wafted everywhere, so much so that everything seemed to be in a haze. Everyone was busy doing something. Normally she would have been there, helping, but her auntie, after seeing her nearly have another seizure, had signaled to everyone to let her be, let her rest. She stared at the trees, letting the smoke fill her, the laughter and talk around her creating peace. Sylvane approached. From far away, Ette could hear her footsteps. She looked up and smiled, nodding her head, wanting her to sit next to her.

She did, quietly, looking out, letting the silence between them sit. Years without words. That's what it was.

"You've changed." Sylvane said, staring at the ground.

"Yeah," Ette responded, wanting to say more, but instead, shook her head, wishing she hadn't. Changed. But knowing that life does that. War swam all over her like a poisoned fish, biting at her insides. She wanted so badly to take Sylvane away to the woods, to hold her there, to cry. She felt her hand tremble, and she put the other one on it to calm it down. She did not dare look at Sylvane but instead changed the subject.

"How was the paddling?" she asked, wanting more than anything to erase everything that happened after the day she left, the Amtrak, and then the plane to Iraq.

"It was good," Sylvane answered, appearing to be glad for the diversion. She glanced at Ette's trembling hand. She did not miss a beat.

"We saw lots of dolphins. They followed us for the longest time."

Her voice was like a song; Ette wanted her to keep talking. She wanted her to tell her everything like she used to, all the stories of her life, holding her, smelling her, stroking all the places that felt like home. Sylvane was home for her. It did not matter what she had said. Just listening to her made her smile.

"It's time to eat," Sylvane said. "I told the pullers I would eat with them. We need to strategize for tomorrow. Dinner and then bed. We leave early tomorrow morning. We thought we would skip S'Kyallup and go all the way to Chileute."

Ette nodded. She was proud of Sylvane. This had been a life's dream for her, to do the Tribal Journey, traveling the way of the ancestors, connecting with her roots, her people, letting her physical and her spiritual body find its strength.

Sylvane got up and joined the food line. She did not look back. Ette winced, wanting so badly for the words to come out. *Damn it!* she said to herself. *Who am I now? I can't even talk anymore.*

She felt her heart sink watching Sylvane move back into the crowd to join her mob. She closed her eyes and remembered that day as if it were yesterday, ten years earlier when she boarded that train from King Street Station in Seattle. Sylvane had begged her not to go. When Ette had gotten the command to join the forces in Iraq, she had gripped the letter and almost tore it up. Sylvane's screams still ricocheted in her mind, imploring her to leave with her to Canada. Her aunt would take them in, letting them stay for as long as they needed to in her cabin way up north in BC, in Haida Gwaii. *There was always room for more in her family. They need you there,* she had pleaded, *and you need to be around your people, our people, living the ancient ways. And we would be together, with no permanent war scars.*

Ette had screamed back. She could not leave the army. It was in her family, her blood. Her people would disown her forever. She had served in the US military for ten years. She could not abandon them now. It was her duty to protect her family's honor. The country.

That's all propaganda. Where is your voice? Who are you? Sylvane had retorted. *What has this country done for you, anyway? You have a brain, and you are not using it.* Her words had spat out like fire, uncontained.

Sylvane left then, slammed the door. She slept at her cousin's that night. And again, the next night and the next. Ette spent those nights bawling like a baby and torn to shreds. Everything had felt like a blur, and her mind had been numb to any truth that could reside in the caverns of her brain. She hated war. She knew that. But that fact kept itself away from her mindless packing, putting things in her duffle while the days crept closer and closer to departure.

She thought of her beloved father, now an ancestor, who would have been proud of her knowing she was serving in a war. He had gone to Korea and came back destroyed from it. He had passed down that mixture of destruction with pride to his one child, his blessed daughter. They never talked of it, but in the gestures of connection, life was about serving one's country, no matter how they treated you. It was just what you did. You did not think, you did not feel, you just did as you were told. The army was your family, and they took care of you.

Ette knew that Sylvane had reluctantly taken the ferry with her that day to the train station. They were silent the whole way, yet they knew what the other was thinking, feeling. When they got off the ferry, walking through the streets of Seattle, Sylvane looked her straight in the eyes.

"You don't have to do this. We could have a good life together."

Ette was silent and slipped her arm around Sylvane, who slithered away like a snake. Ette watched her, there in the street, dry heaves consuming her as she knelt, her face towards the gutter. Then she got up, crying, walking ahead of Ette.

The train was just pulling into the station. It was running late, and the loudspeakers had announced that it would be leaving in three minutes. Ette had grabbed Sylvane, pulling her to chest, kissing her neck, her cheeks, while Sylvane had pounded her back, so hard it made a bruise. She wailed when she held on, gripping Ette one last time, and then pulled away, running, while Ette took her duffle and boarded the train, seconds before it left the station.

Her body, her mind numb, the world zipped by; all she heard was Sylvane's tears, echoing in her mind. The train arrived in Spokane, and for two minutes she stepped outside and had a smoke. She listened to the urban sounds around her, trucks and cars whizzing, and for a second, she imagined Haida Gwaii, the edge of the world, and her feet stuck to the ground, not wanting to get back on this train, and instead take the one back to Seattle. But then a voice inside of her, her father's voice, her uncle's, shouted: *No! Shame on you, buckle up this is your duty, follow it. Life is not about love; it will end up hurting you. Life is about doing what is best for your people, for your country, for your children to feel proud.* Ette tried to shake those voices that were shouting now in her head. She lit another cigarette and exhaled, trying to find her own voice as the train conductor whistled, ready to take off again, and Ette, following orders, got back on the train and slumped in her seat, next to her newly cleaned duffle.

* * *

Ette opened her eyes, smoke wafting around her. Nausea invaded her while she looked around at everyone laughing, eating, enjoying a beautiful summer's evening. Her cousin Siddy sidled up next to her.

"Are you ok, cuz?"

"Yeah, must have been something I ate at lunch. My stomach is feeling sour. Best I go home and get some rest."

"Can I make you a plate, for later?"

"No, that's ok. Think I will skip dinner tonight. Help me to lose a pound, I reckon." She laughed, trying to let family take her mind off memories.

She hobbled off. Pain surged through every bone in her body as her mind felt weak and trembling.

At home, she collapsed onto her recliner and fell quickly into a deep dreamless sleep.

Several hours later, her eyes opened to darkness. She looked over at the clock, seeing it was three in the morning. First light would emerge in a little more than an hour. Ette closed her eyes, feeling their weariness, as memories invaded her brain. She tried to push them away, but they insisted on weaseling a path around her consciousness. Blood everywhere, dismantled bodies lying at her feet, the smell of vomit and excrement invaded her senses. In her head, she heard a cacophonous jumble of wailing and grenades.

Ette halted the images and sobbed. *How did I choose this over love? Is that what it was to be proud, to serve one's country, to protect? I chose this, instead of following the ancient ways, the ways of my people.* She felt disgusted with herself looking at the shadow of the tree outside her window. She got up from her chair, opened the door, and let her feet amble to that tree, the old growth cedar whose branches felt like a woman's arms, holding. She put her own arms around its trunk and let her tears flow, onward and downward, until her entire body was flooded with dampness. She longed to be inside that tree, to release her pain in the flow of sap that nourished itself from within.

The moon was out, and the light beckoned her forward. Her footsteps quiet, she walked through the forest to where the tents were. The pullers were still asleep, waiting for the first light to begin their day's journey. By instinct, she found Sylvane's navy blue tent. Standing outside, she listened to the sounds of her sleep, heavy and full. Ette knew exactly how she slept, the quiet breaths she made when she was deep in slumber. She wanted to unzip the tent and lie next to her, stroke her hair, apologize, start over.

She did not dare wake her. This early morning sleep was the most crucial in letting her paddle that day with infinite strength.

She silently walked away. She began to see that it was hers now, her life, her steps her own in the forest that was calling her.

She sat on her porch, watching the sun rise, endless wisps of light emerging from the darkened sky while the moon filtered its last rays before its timely descent into nothingness.

When the light began to pour through the trees like a finely graded syrup, warming the world, Ette walked to the beach. The pullers, one by one, stepped silently into their canoes. Sylvane caught Ette's eye and walked towards her, her paddle in one hand.

She reached over, kissing her on the cheek, her warm skin melting its way through Ette, like it always had, and always would.

"Look after yourself. OK?" Their gaze locked for a moment, memories of the sweetness they had, the past lacing them for that brief second like a sun burst, waiting for more.

Sylvane walked away, holding her paddle in her arms. She stepped into the awaiting canoe. Settling herself in, the crew paddled away, and Ette stared at them, at the canoe, at the strokes of each turn until they, too, disappeared over the horizon.

When all the canoes were no longer even a dot on the water, Ette hobbled away, stopping at her home to get her drum. She stripped off her clothes. The sweat lodge called her in, as she chanted and prayed and drummed, crying, escaping the confines that had put her there. The cedars welcomed her, as they always did; their thick sweet smell entered her pores, her own drumbeat echoing around her, through her, and away for that entire day and into the night, her body, her mind, her soul a vessel into the infinite. Her people were all there in visions, her ancestors. They chanted with her, through her, their voices melodious and incessant, moaning and screaming her drum still beating, her sweat pouring through her, the stillness of the forest surrounding her always.

THE SMELL OF THE
BURNING VIOLIN

Her long, dark wavy hair with streaks of grey tickled my nose while the blue on her toes dazzled in the sunlight. I often studied the way her mouth moved when she spoke, like the waves, coming and going, sometimes loud and buoyant, crashing and breaking down barriers, and sometimes quiet and fragile, like gentle laps upon the shore. We were both wounded animals coming home to rest. Our common thread was our mysteriousness. Life had eaten us, devoured our quintessential ingredients, and what remained was a need for closeness in our remaining years. I believe that she knew every part of me, knew my thoughts before they were formed, sensed the moment my tears or giggles would come and converge with her's. When she stroked my skin with her warm and velvety hands, she discovered hidden crevices and let me soften into an amorphous world that felt deliciously sweet, allowing me to forget everything that had wounded me. She made me ponder life. She brought me life. I remember staring at her blue toenails for hours sometimes, and, somehow, I would find answers to all the questions that jostled my brain.

I knew Genette wanted me to uncover everything, leaving nothing hidden. Only she could do this with me. One day, she asked me something that would significantly alter the course of my life.

The sun was pouring through the morning clouds, warming our bellies. She had just kissed me on the cheek. Our toes were wet from the incoming tide. I remember purring in her ear, not wanting that moment to end.

"Tell me about your violin," she said, staring at the water.

She turned to face me. For her, there was no space between our gaze and her question, but for me, the signs came up, blazing red. I smelled the smoke again. I shivered, and tears started to pool in my eyes. I closed them, willing her question away.

"How do you know?" was all I could say.

"I saw the case in your hall closet, hidden underneath all those scarves you have. I was looking for my umbrella the other day. You were taking a nap. I knocked on the door, and your housekeeper didn't answer. I just let myself in." She paused. "I had an intuitive feeling that you were hiding a violin from something." She looked in my eyes. I said nothing. I squirmed.

"What is going on?" she asked. Her voice was gentle. She stroked my hair, and watched the tears fall onto her hand, drop by drop.

I sat up abruptly and stared out at the sea. I could tell she knew I wanted her close, but not too close. I closed my eyes. It all came back; after most of my life, locking it tightly in, the story emerged.

When I opened my eyes, the words flowed out.

It began with the fields of daffodils and narcissus. That is when I knew I was in love. It was the end of May 1942. We had met at the Conservatoire, where we played together in a string quartet. We discovered later that we lived on the same street. One Sunday, she invited me on a picnic with her mother and her sister. We drove through winding roads, through towns that became small farms. Rolled up bushels of wheat sat in rows, like sentries in a vast world. Thick forests of pine towered above and beside us, still the road wove itself to the top, to a hillside overlooking the valley of Villard, outside Grenoble. In the distance the Alps blazoned, like turrets of a castle. The air was so fresh that day you could even smell the tender shoots of grass that were growing around us. A perfect sun laced our bare shoulders, and the cool breeze floated around us like a dream, as we laughed and ate cheese, bread, patés and little cakes and drank from the bottle of wine her mother had brought.

If you were to look at a photograph of us, you would not see a trace of worry. All our senses were alive that day. She put her hand on mine as we passed the bottle back and forth. I swooned from the sweetness of her perfume. The smell of musk from a continent away filled my nostrils, urging me to move closer, to get more of her. The sound of her voice was like a tantalizing song, gentle yet pulsing and rhythmical, beckoning me to pull out my violin, like she brought out hers. I let myself fall, sinking into only her, knowing I would do anything she wanted. Her mother and sister sat quietly while Véronique and I played Bach, and then Bartok, followed by Pleyel, and then we ended up with Vivaldi, letting the notes soar over the hill. We were perfectly in tune and in harmony with each other. The energy between us was playful and passionate. It was like a game, a love affair with wood upon wood. When we were done, the applause from her family blended with our smiles. Our laughter echoed. The memory of this moment held me for years to come.

We put our instruments away and then danced through the intoxicatingly sweet fields of yellow and white, picking bunches of flowers. We wrapped bouquets of daffodils around our heads; all four of us were queens for the day. Her cheeks were ripe while she playfully kissed me when her family wasn't looking. Her lips folded into mine like they were always meant to be there. Her scent wafted through me, over me, into me. Her mother turned around, saw us and winked.

As the sun began its regretful descent, we put our things in the car and got ready to leave and return to the city. I glanced over at their belongings sitting in their trunk, odds and ends, and then I spotted them, the sweaters that had been thrown off and tossed in a corner. A yellow six-pointed star had been pinned on each one. Three stars, three cardigans. Three in the family. The father had been long gone.

On the way back, Véronique told me about an orchestra she played in. They were to perform *Carmina Burana* with a full choir on the sixteenth of July in the oldest church in the region of Isère. They needed another violinist, because her stand partner had broken her arm. I loved that piece of music, written in 1936 by Karl Orff, the text in medieval Latin from the eleventh or twelfth centuries.

My violin strapped to my back, the next day I entered the Conservatoire de Grenoble and auditioned for the seat. The conductor smiled after my last note and handed me the part. He told me we would practice every Monday and Wednesday from 7pm to 11pm and on Saturdays from 2pm to 5pm until the concert in the middle of July. I hurried to my seat, next to Véronique, and I dreamily picked up my instrument, feeling the pulse of music, the tantalizing scent of her next to me as I floated into the ethereal range of the notes.

In the beginning of the second week of July, our rehearsals moved into the Church, a fourteenth century gothic edifice that to me deified the goodness in humanity. From the first note we played in that towering mass of stone, there was, for lack of a better word, transcendence. Every sound we made soared to heights that went beyond imagination;

every tone and vibration that was produced from a piece of wood or a piece of metal, or the human voice, was instantly sent into the ethers, moving past boundaries of the mind to the limitless nature of the soul.

As we focused on each note, not wanting to lose our places, I stole glances at Véronique. While playing our violins, letting our bows stroke the strings, creating sounds that traversed into those places of infinity, I saw tears come from her, pools of emotion from her eyes. I, too, felt it, this brilliance, this moment of perfection that embraced our souls, letting us forget the harrowing times of our era, the ugliness right outside the door, in France, in Germany, all over Europe.

On the Wednesday before that Saturday's concert, the choir entered. Three hundred men and women, three hundred voices from all over France ceremoniously walked into the church, wearing regular street clothes, but adorned with voices that spoke to lives lived way beyond that singular moment in time. Somehow, all those people knew what to do, and they organized themselves into places where their voices would be home: sopranos, altos, mezzos, tenors, and basses. All in a few moments they were there, ready, and the baton was raised.

The text, in Latin, *"O Fortuna, vela luna...,"* *"O Fortune, like the moon you are changeable, ever waxing and waning; hateful life first oppresses and then soothes as fancy takes it; poverty and power it melts them like ice...So at this hour without delay pluck the vibrating strings; since Fate strikes down the strong man, everyone weep with me!"* *"...quod per sortem sternit fortem, mecum omnes plangite!"*

On the sixteenth of July, the orchestra, all in black, entered the church when the audience hushed, and in that quiet, the silence echoed up into the spaces of the Gothic heights. The choir, in their crimson robes, seamlessly entered from the nave to the back of us, around us, encircling our instruments. We were all protecting each other at that solemn moment when the conductor arrived, baton in hand. He looked at each one of us and bowed his head, making a silent prayer for humanity.

We began.

In a pungent display of bravado, the sounds we made reverberated to the chambers of the heart; the church and the audience let us describe what music can only express. If only we could all live in this world, if only our music would never stop, this soaring to heights in harmony with each other, we, all of us the witnesses to a peaceful dominion of humans, we the protectors of all mankind in this act of creation, instruments and voices of human workings, making something so beautiful together that felt like love.

When the last note was played, there was silence again. Though this time, the silence had transformed all of us, for there was not a dry eye in that church, and the applause lasted for almost thirty minutes. Everyone stood together one last time, exhausted, but overcome with joy and grief. We felt afraid of leaving that church in the hands of those who did not know the secret that we had just shared, the meaning of life we had conveyed, the cravings we all had for peace.

In the stillness of the night, we all exited the building, our usual banter absent, while cars turned over their engines and soon, the church and the parking lot were completely emptied.

When I kissed Véronique on each of her cheeks, before I got into my parents' car and she stepped into the awaiting car of her mother, there was our usual sweetness, her smell that drew me in, but underneath, I smelled her fear, and mine. At some level we both knew that we would never see each other again.

I could not sleep at all that night. I thought of her violin, I thought of her, and I wanted to run to her home, and into her bed, and hold her, for I knew she was crying and not sleeping. Lying restless, tossing and turning, I saw my own powerlessness, and I realized then that music and our violins were our strength, and beyond that, in the encroaching world, we had nothing; war had reduced us to tiny flecks of dust in a corner.

As the dark of the night crept with disdainful steps into the spaces of what was real, I heard them, with my excellent hearing, labored footsteps on the cobbled stones outside. I jumped out of bed and looked out. With the tiny streetlamp in the distance as my beacon, I saw a long line of people, their dark, tangled hair tossed around, still in their nightclothes, yanked out of their slumbers, their yellow stars emblazoned like fire illuminating their path, invisible to the city that still lay sleeping. There were children, some so small they could barely walk, grown men, trembling, women clutching onto sleeping infants, and old people hunched over, stumbling with each step. I was too far to hear everything, but I saw tears held in, gasps of shock and disgust, as barking men forcefully whispered, thrusting them forward to their predetermined destiny.

Not until many months later it was finally revealed that this walk towards hell was dictated by the Vichy government, who ordered that all Jews be stolen from their homes in the middle of the night, forced onto trains to Paris, where they were eventually then shoved into railway cars headed to Auschwitz and other concentration camps.

While night moved into the minute moments of day, they were gone, like a mirage, and what was left was an empty road, and the streetlamp revealed nothing.

I ran out of my house as the sun rose. I threw myself through the streets, eerie with a silence that made me shiver. I felt rage pulling at my insides, a mass of green bile collected inside my mouth when I smelled smoke coming from the area where Véronique lived.

Holding my belly, I ran to the smell, and there, hearing laughter from young male voices, I saw it, her house, the one next to hers, and the one on the other side, cracking and sputtering, flames emitting from the wooden frames, spewing out into the air, relentless and suffocating. The laughter disappeared, the running footsteps were hidden into the folds of the city, while the fire consumed every bit of her home.

Fire fighters only came at the end, and their sirens roared too late. The skeleton of her house stood there on the street, naked and raped. I stumbled and forced myself to watch. My eyes burned from the smoke, and I began to gag, heaving while the smoke got into my lungs. Then I smelled it, burning wood. I detected a particular smell, that of ancient wood, a maple and spruce, the sweet aroma of varnish. The spruce crackled, and made sparks that flew in the air, up and away, and then vanished. It was death I smelled.

The violin.

I ran inside the burning building. There wasn't anything left, just smoke. I put my hand to my mouth, stifling the fumes. I found the remnants of the front hall closet. Everything had turned to ashes. In the corner of what had been a wall, there was a box. I pushed aside the ashes and saw a mangled violin case. I grabbed it and ran out of the building.

When I got home, I opened it. The violin was gone. All that was left was embers.

For me, the world stopped the day Véronique left, and her violin burned in her home. I never got rid of that case. I never opened it again.

* * *

My life after that became a dizzying haze of nothing I remember. Details obliterated themselves as quickly as they formed, a series of events that I felt no connection to. I was unable to function, talk, and hear; voices were all jumbled and blurred. My days were spent looking out the window and imagining her there, laughing and dancing on that hillside with the flowers around her. All I could smell each day was smoke. My lungs continually felt clogged, and I coughed fitfully every night in my sleep. I barely ate; I was so tiny, a shriveled body encapsulated in grief. I lived with my parents until they died.

During this confusing time where my memory seems to have collapsed, my parents moved the three of us to the coast of California, to an old sprawling home by the sea. I spent each day staring out the window. In my mind I heard Véronique's laughter. It was the only sound that came to my ears.

Forty years somehow passed.

On the sixteenth of July 1982, I woke up. I began to smell something other than smoke. I opened my eyes to the fragrance of the sea and the salt mingled on my tongue. I smelled coffee brewing, freshly baked bread, and I heard for the first time the maid Lucille, in the kitchen, singing. The sun poured through my open window.

I walked over to her and smiled. She stared at me; her mouth dropped open. When she appeared to have grasped the idea that finally I was alive again, she rattled off in French. Until that day, I had forgotten every single word of French. In my forty-year silence, words blurred into a mix of sounds that meant nothing to me. All at once, I rattled back to her in my mother tongue, and together we laughed. She cried, and I did too. She hugged me tightly, and I sank into her softness. I realized she was all I had.

I was sixty years old. When I glanced at myself in the mirror for the first time that morning, I noticed that my hair had turned completely white. My hands were wrinkled, and my eyes were drawn, sinking into the folds of age.

I ran to the waves, and like a child, I jumped and danced in the tide and felt the spray of water. The chill of the Pacific Ocean warmed me from the insides. I looked up at the sky and saw blue for the first time in all those forty years where a smoky grey was the only color that had invaded my obscured vision.

Every day for an entire year, I woke up and let colors, water, sand, trees and the sounds of the breeze fill me. I was hungry, famished, and at every mealtime I devoured everything on my plate, wanting more. An empty vessel, I craved sustenance, and after that year, I began to feel full. My limbs gradually became flexible and strong. I was ready to let life in again."

* * *

I looked at Genette. Her eyes were fixed on mine, and she nodded. Tears fell down her face. She, too, knew murder. Her twin, taken, as she was walking home alone from school one day when she was sixteen, in Auckland, had been raped and slaughtered. I realized at that moment that Genette and I found each other to release something, to ease each of our selves into the spaces of another chapter of our lives.

She tilted her head, silently inviting me to continue. It seemed she wanted more of my story, the present, what happened next.

"In the middle of July," I resumed, "two years after I woke up, there you were. I remember so vividly my walk on the beach, listening to the sound of my own heart beating, the waves accompanying me. Usually, a vacant beach greeted me on those early morning walks. But on that day, you stood, like a beacon, a lighthouse at the far end of the sand,

99

where the two corners of the massive boulders meet, joining the eddies of water flowing in and around them. You looked right at me; you were staring, when I approached. There was no way I could avert your gaze. When I finally met you, you said, "Hi." But it wasn't like a simple "hi," and then on you went. Your "hi" pierced something inside me and burst a bubble. It didn't pop and explode, but rather it sent a warm calming fluid through me. I said "Hi" back. And accompanying that "hi" was a smile. I remember thinking to myself, neither of us is American; how interesting to find each other on foreign soil. But more than that, I recall feeling that my smile was different, it felt like the smile of a child, but one who has grown up without even knowing it."

I paused then. It was no longer my story. I looked in Genette's eyes. It was ours now. Our story. I knew the moment I saw her standing there, blocking my path, that my life would change from that day onward. I sensed that the loneliness that had invaded me for all those years, the smoke-filled reality of obliteration, was ready to come crashing down, dissolving itself into the space of the sea, the atmosphere, the past. And I knew from that moment when her eyes met mine, Genette and I would become one, two beings waiting until the sixth decade of their lives to forge a journey together.

The day of the smile ended after the smile. She walked on. I did too.

The next day, she stood in the same place, looking out to the sea, and as soon as she sensed my approach, she turned towards me, her knowing smile bigger than the day before.

Every day we did this for an entire month. I knew that she knew I was fragile. I knew she was, too. I knew that she knew I would return each day. I could tell she was careful, standing there, meeting my eyes with hers.

A few weeks later, she reached out her hand, and I instinctively took it, feeling its warmth and softness, an invitation to her heart.

One day in the second month of our encounters I sat shivering. The fog had not lifted, and the wind lashed everywhere. She pulled out from her bag an immense woolen blanket. She wrapped its warmth around me, and then around herself. We sat on the sand and cuddled inside, like two foxes in a cave, looking out at the ocean, not speaking but feeling that words had come and gone and what was left was a delicious silence, like a dessert.

She put out her hand, and mine rested in it. While the waves crashed in front of us, I took her hand and reached it up to my lips, kissing it. With salt on my tongue, I looked at her, her eyes soft and dreamy, her gaze went to my heart and asked for more. My lips met her neck, bathing in its salt, and then she edged her face so close to mine that her breath rested on my cheek, and I felt the sweetness of it mingled with something hot, fire. I closed my eyes and shivered. My memories and my story were still hidden and wrapped up in a vault, yet I could tell she sensed something. She reached her arms out and held me, stroking my hair, letting the tears flow. Our cheeks touched.

Raindrops began to fall, gentle at first, but then the storm grew in its voluminous path. When the wind picked up, the waves crashed even harder, spraying us with droplets that turned into larger drops that began to soak our heads. She took my hand and led me to her trailer, there on the beach. Running together we began to laugh, letting the water cascade everywhere, our hair, our toes. We entered her home, and she slammed the door shut. She led me to her bed. We threw off our wet clothes, got under the covers together and she added more blankets. We held each other, curling up into the folds of each other's bodies, while the rain and wind whipped around every crevice of exposed land outside.

In my head, I heard *Carmina Burana*, the tympani smashing, crying out, the voices hauntingly soaring to the heights of the church. I closed my eyes, feeling Genette's warmth surrounding me, tears releasing onto the sheets, her bare skin. In my mind the violins entered, sweetly, like a balm to a wounded landscape, I sighed and let myself sink into the softness of the woman next to me. I pressed myself closer, wanting her, her skin, she, like the violin. Her breath and mine flowed together, harmonies, the voice and the instrument. In our silence, there was a symphony while the rain and the wind outside made the music that blended with our quiet moans, effortless sounds of water and air, fire and earth.

Curled together, lulled, we fell asleep.

Hours later our eyes opened, and the fading sun caressed into the air. It was late, evening already. I readied myself to go, knowing that Lucille would be worried. Genette walked me to my house, and while our eyes promised more, our gaze said good-bye.

Lucille, looking through the curtained windows, saw Genette for the first time, but more, saw our gaze. She knew. She told me I must invite her to tea.

September's fog had lifted, the rain clouds also gone, and as October neared, Genette's footsteps matched the soft autumn sun that bathed her shoulders. Holding a bunch of sunflowers, she entered the space of my glorious home, the one Lucille had told me my parents had fallen in love with when they came to this country, during the war. Wishing to escape from the horrors of France, they had immediately found this paradise on the sea, in California, a place that was in their minds, the dream, where everything was paved with gold. They were both musicians, my father a cellist, and my mother a violist, and for years and years, they played with the San Francisco Symphony. During the concert season they would leave me with Lucille, and drive over Mount Tamalpais and across the Golden Gate Bridge each day for rehearsals and performances. I never went with them. In my painful bubble of silence, I couldn't leave the house.

Genette would be the first person who had ever come to visit me since I was a child in France.

* * *

The sunflowers sat gracefully on the table, announcing a celebration. Lucille bounded around the house, herself a joyful bouquet of loveliness. I sat and smiled, watching the happy exchanges between the two women, feeling an intrinsic part of something important, the first time I had felt a part of anything since that afternoon I played my violin in the church.

Genette came often to my home after that day, at first invited as a guest, and then, while autumn progressed, she began to blend in with each corner of the house, and the three of us heard ourselves laugh throughout many an evening. Lucille pulled out recordings that my parents had made with the Symphony and with the well-known "Quatuor du Pont Doré" string quartet that they formed. Genette brought back my parents. I stared at their photos, outlining their faces with my fingertips. I had no memory of their deaths, and now, I longed for their lives, their music, in this house with the ceilings so high. I imagined the acoustics; the church came to my head, soaring up to skies that held notes with a protective feeling of grace.

Every day Genette and I walked on the beach. It was our time to talk, and our time to be silent, to feel connected to the sand and the waves, the salt of the water on our tongues. Since it was now winter, we rarely let our toes touch the freezing tide. We often walked on the bluffs, the ruggedness of the coastline matching the necessity of survival in a tarnished world. The reds and oranges of the succulents melted with the greens and blues of the grasses and sky, colors everywhere reminding us of rejuvenation, when the jagged rocks seemingly erupted from the soft, rich earth, softened by the rain. Down below, sea life, invisible to the human eye, was ever present, while occasional bursts of whale breath spouted up.

With each day, I felt relaxed. My limbs felt supple now, my heart open. I felt seen, heard. Our lips touched often now, blending with the landscape, longing mixture with the sweet breath of home. We now shared everything we had always wanted to share with another, our dreams, our visions, our bodies, our minds.

It was on one of those days, when colors blend, when the sea and sky come together, creating something whole, that she asked me to tell my story, letting me finally toss the key. It was springtime again, and the sun had reemerged. Orange poppies were bouncing around us everywhere.

When the words were done, my story released, I sat still, listening to the seals playfully calling out to each other.

We both scanned the horizon and stared at the air surrounding us. It was as if a breath had been taken, as if we could see the smoke from the burning violin finally escape from the confines of the human heart.

"What allows a person to finally come out of their own vault of pain?" she asked.

I sat quietly, wanting her to continue.

"You and I, we each have spent most of our lives locking away our own horror stories."

"I had to wake up; so did you. I suppose somewhere inside of us there is a voice that tells us when we are ready to escape our own coma. And then that small voice becomes audible, and we walk away, step by step."

Genette took my hand, and put it on her heart, letting me feel the stable beat of it, the reassuring rhythm of a softened soul. We were quiet then, two beings feeling stilled, journeys of life completed, another one yet to be discovered.

"I shall play again," I announced, after a long time of silence.

"Mmm?" she answered.

"Yes. In San Francisco. There is a group of musicians looking for violinists to play *Carmina Burana* in Grace Cathedral this summer."

Genette looked at me. Tears had formed, dropping to her shoulders. Looking at her, I, too began to cry, but for different reasons. With those tears, we both felt old, and yet young; lives ended and began.

Our hands interlacing, each finger fitting around the next, we looked up into the azure spaces of the sky. The pelicans swooped over us, dozens of them, a perfect geometric design forming the letter "V", their bodies free and unencumbered, while our bodies, hers and mine, folded into the other, a melting away of pain, the sun filtering around us, seeping inside.

STRAWBERRIES

There were strawberries everywhere. Luscious and bulbous, so ripe they were oozing sweetness. When Amelia entered the kitchen, the scent overpowered her. She was beyond hungry, and she wanted to devour something sweet, something to erase everything that had enveloped her over the past year.

Her body ached all over, her mind was jumbled in a fog; she had not been as exhausted as this all her life. The doctors called it fibromyalgia. She had just come from the library and had done research on what this was exactly. She had found books written by doctors and even one from a psychotherapist who advocated yoga and other types of self-care to heal from this debilitating condition that often stems from intense grief and loss. She thought of her dad, who passed away in front of her eyes the same day as the woman she wanted to marry looked at her with daggers. She wanted to run as far as possible, away from everything, from loving, from the falling that she loved to do, where she would land in the arms of someone to hold her.

"Catch me, Daddy!" she remembered screaming out when she was two years old in the swimming pool that day, her cowlicks sticking up from her head with abandon. He was always there, arms open, ready to grab her before she drowned in the abyss of childhood.

Forty years later there was her round face, her sleek body like a goddess. They created a world together, a utopian existence, where no one could come in and destroy their sublime love. One day the knives came out of her eyes, out of nowhere, "a change of heart" she had said. Her face had spewed out hatred that was most likely reserved for someone else but somehow landed on Amelia in the middle of the living room that day while they were eating, for the last time, vanilla ice cream with berry sauce poured over.

* * *

Amelia took a whiff of the strawberries, her feet still at the threshold of the kitchen. The recently mopped linoleum floor was slippery and shiny. She took off her shoes, and like an octopus, she slid amidst the ooze of the detergent. In her frenzy, her arm knocked all the strawberries to the floor, and she continued to slide now through red rubies that mushed under the weight of her feet. She could tell that oxytocin was filtering through her brain, because all pain in that moment was obliterated. She felt inebriated by an iridescent haze, an invitation to the innermost regions of delight. She tumbled into a mysterious place of luxury on the kitchen floor. *Please let me stay here forever*, she mumbled to herself.

Her hand reached out, her long arm like a tentacle with suction cups. She picked up a still intact strawberry, and her delicate fingers wrapped around the Rubenesque jewel. She gently brought it close to her nose, letting her tongue slip and slide around the contours while she gasped, her entire being filled with an urgency to bite into this piece of wonder.

Finally, longing in her every pore to do this one act, to eat this perfect strawberry held against her lips, finally, her teeth, her fine white enamels found their home in the redness as the juices poured down her chin, frolicking this way and that, in a chaotic embrace of her face. Her teeth became like fire, consuming each morsel, wanting another just as soon as one slid down her throat. One more, just one more bejeweled delicacy must be devoured, for the fire would not subside, while another and another perfectly formed strawberry entered the slippery mass, her saliva an entrance to the cavernous folds of her digestive system.

Dozens of these womanly shaped fruits had entered her and filled her in a place of contented satiation while she refused to move from the kitchen floor. She closed her eyes, smiled and slid down to a prone position. Sleep drifted into her, sleep so sweet that it allowed her quite quickly to dream.

As her feet twitched, and her hands shook with abandon, her rapid eye movements beckoned her alpha sleep state, the realm of dreams... She had, in her hand, a strawberry that was as big as a face, a cherubic face so lovely and loving that she held it to her chest like a gift, protected and cherished. There was light everywhere, an effusive luminescence that poured in from every corner of the room. She stared at her grand sized strawberry, recognizing in its contours the face of her betrothed, and she kissed the redness fully, feeling its softness on her lips. She felt so light in her steps as she danced around the room, holding the fruit to her breast. When she finished dancing, she glanced over, and there on the floor in front of her lay a corpse, the form of her father, yet on his face there was a smile, and he was grinning as if he was still alive. She shuddered, and doing so, her giant strawberry transformed, and the angelic face on it became blank, whereupon the fruit in her hand shriveled up and vanished. She looked over and the face of her father also lost its features. She

The rapid eye movements ceased, her twitching quieted, and
Amelia, on the floor of her kitchen, opened her eyes and wondered
how it was she was on the floor surrounded by a dazzling decorative
display of red, almost as if it was all choreographed, a perfect art form.

She took a deep breath, absorbing her dream, this place on the
floor, surrounded by strawberries. She noticed that her body felt alive,
no trace of pain anywhere, the first time she had felt this in more
than a year. She recalled the giant strawberry from her dream, and she
chuckled out loud, the face of her lover, then the face of her father,
smiling, as if he, too, was happy for his youngest daughter. She noted
that she experienced a release in her mind, her psyche, her body, like
she had, in this dream, let go of the noose that had held her viciously
in pain for the past year.

While she sat and took in everything around her, she felt sublimely
calm. From her feet to her head, and inside her heart there was a gentle
beating, like a djembe, making sounds that echoed off the neighboring
hills to the valleys and tundra, far away.

She felt a vibration in her side pocket. It went on and on. In her
blissful state she at first ignored it, and when it wouldn't stop, she returned to the practical world, realizing it was her cell phone on vibrate,
sending her a message. She reached in her pocket and pulled out her
phone, seeing there was a text from her sister.

*"I am at Trader Joe's. How many bottles of champagne do you need?
I forgot what you told me the other day."*

Suddenly everything made sense to her. The strawberries her sister had brought in, just that morning, from the farmers' market. That evening they were to celebrate the announcement of the publication of her picture book entitled "Strawberries in the Closet." For ten years, she had written and submitted novels, short stories, essays, and most recently children's books. Finally, her writing would be published! She had a path now, and tonight, in that very kitchen, all her friends of thirty years and her family would be celebrating with her.

She leapt to her feet, gathering handfuls of the crimson blessed jewels, and she smeared them all over her arms and legs and her face. Strawberry jam enveloped her body while she danced around the kitchen singing Leonard Cohen's "Hallelujah," switching to Handel's version, ending with "Amazing Grace," her voice a sonorous echo reaching the mountains, hundreds of miles away.

"Bring as many bottles as you'd like," she wrote back. Then she added, *"Oh, please bring more strawberries."*

THE LETTER

The letter arrived today. Plain white envelope, a slim piece of paper inside. I could not bear to open the seal, the sticky part holding lost dreams, like the gum of a tree, sap oozing out, a thick mass of intricate fibers.

I remember my first rejection letter. I was only eighteen, and youth poured through me like a pulsing rainstorm, gullies flooded with water, and underneath, everywhere there were things growing, spilling out. She was there, the one who made my heart fly, the one I still have visions of. She opened the mailbox for me, grabbing onto what we later burned on the full moon.

Decades later, I would drop another one in the cedar chest that held hundreds more. Then, I wore comfortable shoes, a purple, tattered scarf. I had buried two husbands, a son, and ten dogs. My brain vacillated between epitaphs and soliloquies. Some people in town called me wise. Most thought I was crazy. I did not care. Still, I wrote.

Yesterday, the doctor told me I had two weeks left to live. Today, I held the envelope in my hand, shaking, thinking of each word submitted, my life completely unveiled as I, the naked soul, stood shriveled and housed in a body of infinitely decaying particles.

I ripped open the seal. I cut my finger, and watched the white paper turn red, my own diseased blood smearing the page. Raindrops began to fall and blurred the print into a tangled web of words. I headed inside; my legs felt weak. I had done this before, witnessed the fall of the heart from a slim piece of paper. I wanted to sleep, and my mind craved oblivion.

Instead, my eyes burst open, drawn to something, hope maybe. Through the dampened muddle, they zoomed to the first line: *Congratulations!*

BIRTH

My umbrella dropped pools of water all over the hard, wooden bench. Her eyes dazzled the room. Her man sat next to her, touching her bare skin. Even her shoes glistened, when she told him she was so nervous she could hardly breathe.

I have been told all my life not to stare, yet my eyes could not focus on anything else but her presence. I wanted to study happiness, feel all the pores of someone who is bleeding joy.

When my number was called, I ventured toward the birth certificate window, next to this stranger, at the same time she and he signed their names and waited to go upstairs to the chambers of awe, the rings in his pocket, gently wrapped in silk.

The rain continued outside, and the wind whipped the wintered trees, while my eyes continued to gaze at her shoes, her silky skin, the ebullient smile that emanated from her face.

While I was awaiting the piece of paper that reminded me of my birth, all I could think about was running away.

Pain ricocheted down my neck, pulsing to my back, and nausea crept in like a widowed soul. I have loved someone. I remembered it. The room spun while she floated in my mind, her dark hair wrapped around her thick lashes. I would have done anything for her.

At first, she led me down the trail, through the thickly wooded cedar forest, our backdrop for the kisses she placed on the back of my neck, and then over to my ears. She let me believe that love can truly happen in our lifetimes. She let me see that love was fearless. Her dragon met my tiger, and from that, sublime waves met each other in tangible acts of courage. She showed me how one must love oneself before loving another, the soul a weathered, yet tender being.

Time passed. I do not really know how long. One day the words came out of her mouth, gently, decisively:

"I can't."

Then she slipped away, silently, through those still hushed woods, like a deer, vanishing after that, the poof after a flame blown out.

* * *

The clerk returned with the piece of paper, stamped and official, reminding me of the day I came into this world, the moment I cried out at the hugeness of it all, leaving the warmth of my mother, life embodied in those first few seconds, spread out on wrinkled fingers and toes. I wonder if my soul wondered if I would love, if I would ever be loved.

I walked out of the whitened building towards the train station wanting to take that piece of paper with the emboldened fanciness, and shred it, tossing the pieces in the frenzied wind that encompassed me. I had to force myself not to, while I let the rain soak into my feet, and I felt the chill run down my neck, reminding me of life, my own pathos, but also perhaps a certain brilliance of it that belonged just to me.

I took a breath, and, upon the exhale, I remembered everything she had told me there in the woods in the space that was once ours. On the street, I began to feel this indescribable piece of lace surrounding me, a whisper in the wind, a sweet future that suddenly awaited me, flying over the nearby train tracks, flying against that wind, sweetly coming towards me.

DANCERS

She stood outside on the porch while the October heat lingered. The smell of a distant wildfire invaded her nostrils. Delicate ashes laced the ground. She looked through the large picture window. No one noticed her smiling; no one even noticed her. Perhaps she never wanted this moment to end, or perhaps she wasn't even in the moment at all, but ensconced in some reverie, where time was inconsequential. Still, she smiled, an observer. She stroked her ring finger, forgetting that the day before her husband died, the day before the snake's rattle had consumed the only man she had ever loved, her wedding ring had fallen off her emaciated finger, and silently slipped to the ground, disappearing into the folds of obscurity.

The three sisters, grown women now, stood opposite the two sisters, no longer little girls. Yet, the five were all like children in that glimpse of time, and their dresses gently sashayed around their bodies. The klezmer music invited them all: clarinets and accordions, somewhere a distant fiddle, beckoned shoes to get thrown off, bare feet touching the rug, their grandmother's and great grandmother's rug, and the hardwood floor, where they stomped to the pulsing rhythms of something nebulous, yet something hopeful, some translucent memory from their past.

She, the matriarch, smiled and sighed. She had never once cried in her life, not for sadness, not for joy. Once, a psychiatrist had told her he had never seen someone hold in so much emotion. Looking at her family, hearing the stomping, watching the frenzy around her, there could have been tears. So many things jumbled in her head while she watched her people, the joy on their faces. The dance enveloped all. Isn't that a mother's wish to see her children dance around her mother's living room, peeking the dust spill up from the floorboards? Even her withered body, the folds of arthritis that ate away at her spine, her legs, her hands, even that body could have danced at that moment.

Where did she go, in her reveries? She had witnessed so much. She was back there, nine years old, on the cold cement floor of her basement; she did not want to be alone. Her baby sister was sleeping. She wanted to wake her. Somewhere inside of her, though, she told herself that alone was where she had to be. It would be a theme that would get played out in her life. The theme of survival. But then, she could not have known this. Then, there were bombs. Then, the war had just broken out. She remembered having to pee; she was not allowed to. She wanted to run to the swing outside but outside was now forbidden. She was a prisoner, and childhood was now a maimed passage of her life.

She did not dance until her wedding twenty years later to the man who would take her away, the knight on his horse, she used to say. Where was he now, when all the little girls danced in front of her? He should have been there, taking pictures, holding her hand. In the middle of the night sometimes, there were those dreams; the bombs never went away. He could never know what it was like, but always he held her hand until her breath came back. The first of September 1939 would never leave her memory.

Their eyes were all so dark. She had never noticed how dark they were. So mysterious. Her girls. Her granddaughters. When had they become so beautiful? When had they learned to dance so well, their bodies so lithe, twisting and turning, twisting and turning? It made her dizzy! She thought she was going to fall. Only memories seemed to hold her these days. She remembered the ashes in the air, bodies burning, her aunt, screaming. She remembered Hitler's voice on the radio. The voice of hatred. Why was his voice coming back to her now, when the music around her reminded her of a braided round challah on the New Year?

She put her hand to her heart, to remind herself that she was still breathing. *Why am I still here,* she wondered? She touched her hand; it felt so cold. She thought she felt his hand grasp hers. He still had his wedding ring on. It had not slipped off his finger like hers did. Her body trembled. Each time he did this, slip his hand in hers, she had what the doctors called a psychogenic seizure. They gave her all kinds of drugs to stop it from happening. Said it wasn't good for her brain. She took the pills, still wanting him back, secretly wanting his hand in hers, never leaving.

The autumn after he died, she went to the edge of the ocean to do a Tashlich; she threw breadcrumbs in the water and watched them float away. Little minnows had grabbed at the crumbs and took them. They had always done this together, at the beginning of the new year. They used to laugh doing it, because they had no transgressions they could think of. He would grab her then, after watching the tiny breadcrumbs float in the water. He would grab her and kiss her, and she would laugh. After he died, she stopped doing it. She stopped being able to walk, her head drawn now, her legs more useless by the day.

Why am I thinking of that? She wondered, the twirling dervishes spinning on her mother's wooden floor, their dark hair like a mass of birds' nests, buoyed by their movements.

They all took care of her; she was, after all, the matriarch. She never did like queens, though, and she scoffed at the notion that they had given her that title. When he vanished, they had all put the crown on her head, and she shuddered underneath her smile. She would rather rest her head on his chest than wear that gilded emblem of authority.

She stared at the youngest one, the most dazzling of the pack, a mere nineteen years old and still in the throes of wonder. She could have been like that, too, had September the first never happened. She always had her brain in the clouds before that day.

Her head began to pulse and throbbed while the clarinet played. In her mind, the bombs returned, as they often did in moments of sweetness. She could never hold onto those moments; her memories posed like thieves in her spirit. She had detested the star she had to wear on her sleeve. She had torn it off several times. Each time, her mother had sewed it back on.

She started to wheeze. Usually when this happened, someone would rush over and give her the inhaler. She could not stand that stuff, and besides no one was there now to pump her up with steroids. No one was even noticing her. Her breathing quieted. She realized then that it was not about her, it wasn't about her dead husband, in that moment it wasn't about anyone at all, while the feet spun, and the dancers laughed.

She smiled again; her feet felt light, like they had wings. She felt like she had died and there she was, ready to soar away from what had gripped her. With her walker, she ambled away from the porch window, her head held high. Rolling towards the door, she entered the room. The beat of the accordion fit perfectly in her heart valves. There, on the rug, the rug her parents had bought in Turkey, she rolled. The wheels of her walker spun out of control, when she abandoned the vehicle and threw her hands up. Her face lit up like fire. The women, the dark-haired beauties she called her family, circled around her, and they clapped their hands in the air and threw her kisses, making her the center of their dance, while she stood and rocked from side to side, her legs strong and firm, her heart a miracle of rhythm.

Tears flowed from her like a foreign language. Everyone saw it, everyone noticed but her. They witnessed this miracle, their mother, their grandmother smiling and crying in the center of their circle.

The music stopped. The CD had come to an end. Even the distant violin was hushed. The women sat down, their breaths labored. Everyone sat except her, the matriarch. She stood, still in the middle, and held up her hand, ready to speak, dresses splayed out on the floor, surrounding her. She was quiet, while she gathered her thoughts. Then it was her mother who entered her vision, and stood there in the living room, her hand up, just like her daughter's was now. *Ah, she gave speeches, my mother, words people listened to, her hand raised just so, all eyes focused on the smallness of my mother's body, the commanding presence. No, she thought. I am not my mother. I am not a matriarch. I have nothing to say, and here I stand, in my mother's living room, my family all around me, and where is he, my husband? Where is my voice, oh where?*

She closed her eyes, and there he was, dancing with her, whirling her in a circle; there was no such thing as loss, when he twirled her around and she laughed, just laughed. Five sets of eyes stared at her, her body limp, twitching.

"Mom!" they yelled, their voices fraught.

She did not respond; she was smiling, dancing, happy for the first time in years. There were so many things she had not told him. She had nagged him incessantly, *why had I done this?* Her thoughts began to evaporate. She did not want to heed the incessant calls from her family to return. He was saying goodbye. He was giving her one last spin, and then he said he had to go. Her ebullient face became blank, her color turned ashen when she opened her eyes, her family there; worried expressions greeting her.

"I am so tired," she said in a tiny voice, after staring at them blankly.

They led her to her bed, her legs shaky, her mind confused. She fell into a deep sleep and tossed and turned. She did not know where she was. In the middle of the night, in her sleep, she stroked his pillow, her hand grazed over the softness of the cotton.

They say a person chooses their death, the exact time they are ready to leave. She was in that place, the pendulum swung over her heart, *it is my time, it is not my time,* back and forth it swung. To the right, it was yes. To the left, it was no.

* * *

Hushed voices came from all corners of the house. No one slept that night. They all knew their mother and grandmother was on the precipice; one foot, dangled with them, one foot, dangled with the other world. The spell of the dance was broken, shards of memories filled their skulls, their brains now on fire while they contemplated the end. They could never know her world, for they were only the children and grandchildren of hers. They had never heard bombs; they had never smelled a body gassed. Their dance spoke of their innocence, and now, it, too, was silenced.

There was an unspoken voice that night that yearned for more. A strong, collective voice that counteracted the one that claimed, "The party's over." Had they asked her all the questions they needed to ask? Did they even know her? Had they taken her for granted, all those years, assuming she would always be there? Without even knowing it, they had allowed her silence; they had all been taken care of by her,

her stories hidden in the folds of her now wrinkled skin. They had not beckoned them out. Moments earlier, they had all, they thought, been free, when their feet caressed the floor, when they leapt in the air, when their smiles radiated in that room while the music enveloped their souls. They were five women, bonded by blood, and there was love that pulsed in that bond, as well as in their hands that grasped for stars in the sky.

Now, no matter, there was a woman who gave life to all of them, who was in the bedroom at the other end of the house, contemplating leaving them all.

It was the youngest ones, it always seems to be the youngest ones, who knew. From all the whispers, and all the tears and all the angst of those women in dresses—who were acting more like girls than women, who still needed a mother and always would—two leaders emerged. These young women had traveled the world, had learned multiple languages and had made it their passion to help refugees. They were the granddaughters, who somehow knew about suffering. Somewhere in their DNA they smelled the horrors of what had happened to their beloved grandmother, and with that knowledge that had seeped into their pores they approached the bedroom where she was still sleeping, still teetering on the edge of life and death.

The three older ones followed, standing like sentries at the threshold, watching. They witnessed the younger ones, no longer children, brush the hair away from the old woman's face, letting in light, but more than that, in that brushing of the bangs from the forehead, those two transmitted a message to the sleeping aged woman, whose face seemed peaceful. She looked no longer alive, but her heart was still beating.

What was that message? What could they have told her? Those two had sat at the bedsides of those who were dying. They had sat at the bedsides of those who were living. In their youth, they already knew about transitions, about choices. They already knew about love.

Then, they chanted. Soft murmurs came from their throats, deep down, like the roots of a tree, planted for generations, the melodies in a minor key of their ancestors flowed out of them. Their voices were lovely and pure, directed at the heart of the woman who shared their blood, and who, in their songs, shared their stories. Their voices took the form of a dance, a part of their lives, the inter-weaving of history and the present, the melodic frame of devotion, one heart to the next.

They looked at their grandmother and saw tears lightly cascade from the corners of her eyes, gentle wisps of moisture flowing down onto her soft skin, cascading into the wrinkled folds of time.

They sighed, their song ended, the dance and music wrapped around all of them like a protective shield. All the women now stood in a semi-circle around the bed, that same bed that had brought forth the three daughters, that same bed that housed laughs and screams and the thrusting energy of life.

The full moon poured in through the window, and landed on a tea-cup, illuminating it, a halo on an otherwise dark night. All five women, their dresses touching, shimmying even, rocked back and forth, while they silently stared at the cup, their talisman, and gazed, their eyes soft and warm, at the woman in the bed, watching her breath rise and fall.

THE ORANGE RAINCOAT

The bright orange waterproof jacket hung loosely over the chair in the kitchen; the rain was falling hard outside. Day after day creeks rose, rivers gushed, and even the eleven chickens hid under the thick brush, waiting for the storm to abate.

I wondered whether to go outside. The dogs needed a walk; so, did I. I ended up staring at the orange raincoat, gazing out the windows, letting the flatulence of the black lab asleep next to me filter throughout the room.

I felt immobilized and the rain made me sleepy.

Maybe I should take a nap, I thought. *Maybe I will just succumb to the day, the dark skies, the quiet.*

But even the comfy couch in the living room felt too far away. I would have to get up from this hard bench. Besides, the dog's paws were stretched out on my legs, trapping me.

I sighed, feeling my eyelids getting heavier and heavier. They began to close, and when I forced them open, a mouse scurried across the floor. It was of an unusual color. Not your typical grey, nondescript mouse, but rather, it was sheer black with a stunning orange streak running down its body.

I had left the bread out earlier that day. *It must have smelled that*, I thought. It scampered fast through the kitchen, seemingly oblivious to me or to the sleeping, farting dog. It scurried up the cabinets onto the counter, where it encountered the fresh loaf that lay waiting, its enticing smells too hard to avoid.

I wanted to gasp, run, and chase it away. But instead, I sighed and watched it eat. Its whole body was invested in this delectable meal and with its super strong claws, it dug a hole inside the loaf, and there it feasted, devouring the rich grains and seeds.

We humans have been socialized not to like mice, to be afraid of them. And, I admit, I was for much of my childhood. But in that instant, I became fascinated by this little being and its serious investment in good food.

I agreed with this animal.

It *was* a delicious loaf of bread.

* * *

I continued to stare, mesmerized by the flash of orange that came from within the loaf of bread. I knew it wasn't a normal thing for a mouse to have such a color. I read once that there was what's called a free state pygmy mouse native to South Africa. I always thought this name was quite intriguing. This mouse was entirely orange, though, not a black mouse with an orange streak. I pulled out my phone and read that there are orange mice called "shaded mice" that people have as pets, that carry a gene that can lead to obesity and other unhealthy conditions. *No, my mouse looked perfectly healthy.* And then, I continued my web search, and discovered there was a hazel dormouse, an animal who lives in Wales. They can be orange in color, too. But all orange.

But I was *not* in Wales. I was in Scotland.

And I was perplexed.

I knew there was something about my orange-streaked mouse that

I needed to know. I felt obsessed by this animal. I called my secretary, told her I had turned orange, or something of that nature, and asked her to cancel all my appointments that day.

"You turned orange?" she asked, mocking me, I think.

"I don't know. Something orange has come over me, and I need to take a day off to figure it out."

"Maybe you need a doctor?" She paused. "A psychiatrist?"

Now she really *was* making fun of me.

"No, it's just me. You've known me for so long."

"What *am* I going to do with you?" I noted a hint of flirtation in her tone.

"*Rien. C'est trop tard,*" I retorted in French. Nothing, it's too late.

She had heard that line from me so many times over the past twenty years.

* * *

I was then distracted by scampering tiny feet across the counter, over to the sink, down the other counter. Still apparently oblivious to my presence, the little black mouse raised its head in the air, gave a sniff, and then squeezed its body and disappeared into the small crack in the wall.

I began to panic. I needed to follow that mouse. I needed to know where it was going next. I wanted desperately to be a tiny speck, able to slip into the crack in the wall. I despised my large, encumbered body, my humanness, my inability to squeeze and shrink myself.

The dogs were asleep, but when they sensed my panic, they abruptly woke up, and the large one began to bark. The little one became agitated, and the two easily roused themselves from their relaxed place and demanded to go outside. When I opened the door for them, they refused to go out without me, and now both were barking, whining, and howling, and they sounded like they had been neglected for months.

I put on my orange rain jacket, my wellies, and my hat, grabbed the leashes, and opened the door while the dogs bolted outside, into the rain. They immediately ran to the outside wall of the house and began to sniff and sniff, desperate to locate the smell they had detected.

I quickly realized they were sniffing the part of the house that was directly connected to where the mouse had made its exit, from the inside. I wondered why they had no reaction to the mouse's adventures in the kitchen, minutes earlier. I was frightened they would find it, mangle it, and kill it in their perpetual need for a toy to play with.

"Now don't you hurt that little mouse," I heard myself say, realizing full well that those words would most probably not even be listened to.

Just then, a streak of blazing turmeric ran out of the building and rushed into the bushes. The dogs, not missing a beat, ran to these bushes in a passionate chase.

"NO!" I yelled, while the dogs dug themselves deeper into the thick brush, their noses pulling towards the soft, muddy earth.

I felt myself sweat profusely chasing the dogs who were chasing the mouse through the greens and browns that were tangled together.

Every now and then I saw balls of color. I could tell the mouse was smarter than the dogs, because soon after, the dogs returned to me, with nothing in their mouths, and no evidence of anything that had just been masticated.

I heaved a sigh of relief, and I felt something shift inside of me, some kind of energy that I had never noticed in myself.

I felt something creative well up inside, an unexpected orange passion that directed me to get out my paints, my easel, my violin, my lump of clay and make something, create something.

The course of my life at that moment had changed. I could feel it rise and boil inside me, while the light shifted, and a new, even more powerful storm had begun.

I vowed to myself to continue this search for my mouse who had now gone underground and was safe in the expanse of the earth, when I, with my dogs, ventured inside to the warmth of the house.

* * *

The next day I woke up with the first light, something I rarely do, and I bounded out of bed and ventured to the kitchen. I half expected my mouse to be waiting for me with a cup of coffee and a freshly baked scone with jam and cream.

The kitchen was empty. The loaf of bread from the day before, that I had purposely left out, had not been touched. It appeared that my mouse was gone. Society expects humans to heave a sigh of relief when a mouse exits a house, but I felt devastated. My enthusiasm for life dwindled away in front of my eyes. My world seemed grey all over again.

I looked at my hungry dogs, who were eagerly awaiting breakfast, then a walk. I scooped the kibble from the container into their bowls. Their voracious energy while they ate annoyed me. I was still angry with them. I believed they had chased away my mouse, my precious little mouse.

When their kibble had been devoured, they looked at me and then their leashes, and then back at me, with their rhythmic wagging tails.

"I am not happy with you two." I stared at them. "You chased my mouse away."

Their tails continued to wag.

They ignored my words.

Dogs have such a one-tracked mind.

I wanted nothing to do with the canine species. All I wanted was my rodent.

* * *

I thought I would see my mouse on the walk. Scooping up slimy dog poo with my little plastic bag, I kept my eyes focused on the brush, hoping for an orange streak. Green and brown felt overwhelming. All I wanted was orange, my orange. In just twenty-four hours orange had become the only color for me.

In the large field beyond the woods, I methodically threw the ball for the dogs; they raced and caught it, dutifully bringing it back to me. I used to love this game, their enthusiasm, the repetitiveness of it all.

Now, it seemed utterly boring and monotonous, an exercise that utilized absolutely no brain. It seemed a completely pointless game.

My dogs seemed so dependent on me to amuse them. Where I adored this once, now it repulsed me.

After what seemed like hours, but was, in fact, probably just fifteen minutes, the dogs showed disinterest in the fetch game. I was relieved. We all sauntered home. Each of us had his mind on something entirely different. The big dog seemed serene and trotted against my side. The little one, off leash, bounded through the bushes and the riverbank, an endless bundle of joy in the discovery of everything around him. I was the morose human, who trudged silently along, with heavy steps, barely noticing the surging water from the river after the hard rain the night before.

* * *

Had I been paying more attention and had not been so consumed in the perseverance of my woes, I would have noticed something in the bushes. But I didn't notice anything until my little dog disappeared in the grass by the rushing river. He did that often; he obliterated himself in the throngs of anything living and moving, anything alive or dead, and above all, anything edible or even inedible, if he could put it in his mouth and proudly carry it, crunch it, and/or hold it regally between his sharp teeth.

Usually, I did not pay much attention to his antics. He seemed to have a very durable digestive system, and because of that, I let him go on with his canine prowess. It seemed that he had an obsession with power, and he obviously took this matter very seriously.

While the big dog maintained her serene gait next to me, the little one came back with something dangling from its mouth.

Probably a stick, I thought. He was like a furniture mover and seemed to like to displace sticks from one end of the forest to the other.

I quickly snapped out of my dull ache, when I noticed that indeed he was not carrying a stick in his mouth. What emerged from his jowls was a black tail, a long skinny protrusion.

I knew in an instant that inside my dog's mouth, inside the mouth that could NEVER be forced open once something had gone in, was a mouse, *my* mouse.

"NO!" I yelled. "Open that mouth!"

He looked at me with pride about catching something alive, holding it prisoner, biting into it.

"Open that mouth. NOW!"

He looked at me.

Then, he did what I never thought he would do.

He obeyed me.

He opened his mouth and spit out the contents of what was his prey and placed it at my feet.

Then he scampered away, looking oh so happy with himself.

There, at my feet, was a mangled streak of orange, a tiny body that laid limp on the ground.

It was dead.

I screamed.

My precious mouse was dead, killed mercilessly by a dog who thought it was just some playful little toy, something that would make him feel that much better and stronger on this planet.

I picked up the listless being, who, just 24 hours earlier, was ensconced in a loaf of fresh bread, sitting on the counter.

My heart sank while I stroked its thin body and felt the soft down of its still warm fur.

I began to look for a place to dig a hole in the ground.

My fingers noticed a gentle, slow beating coming from the inside of the animal.

"HE IS NOT DEAD!!" I yelled at the trees.

I stroked the wounded being in my hands, my fingers a gentle salve on the fragile mass of neurons that lay deep under the fur.

"We are all such delicate beings," I muttered. "At any given moment we all could die, too."

My tears slid down my cheeks and landed on the mouse. I felt moisture on its fur when I held him close to my chest.

The four of us headed home. It began to rain again, a hard cold rain while we entered the warm house, and the flash of orange in the palm of my hand moved ever so slightly, like a tiny beam of light in a darkened tunnel.

SKIN

I lay in my lover's bed. I felt softer that night; my skin was supple and youthful. I wasn't used to this feeling. I hadn't paid much attention to my body in years, except for what hurt.

I listened to the water from the shower across the hall. Then it stopped. My heart quickened, yet it felt perfectly relaxed, as I waited for the bathroom door to open, and listened to footsteps pattering on the floor.

Five years earlier, I had written a poem that was published in a journal of COVID poetry. In that poem, I envisioned a final call to the pandemic, and I imagined screaming at the top of a mountain, signaling an end to the insanity our world had been experiencing. I also imagined our tongues dancing, mine and that of the woman whose footsteps now slid across the threshold to her bedroom. She threw the towel covering her head onto the end of the bed, slipped under the covers and wrapped her legs around mine.

Just the day before, I was wondering how we humans manage the toxicity that now invades our brains, making us so often overwhelmed. I so often felt lost in the miasma of destruction that our species was creating for each other. Sometimes it felt like we were mere skeletons, walking through brambles and calling this life.

When our lips touched that night, each of us begging for more,

I knew we had been thrown into some moment in history that felt centuries old. Something primitive called and ushered us together, something that went way beyond the here and now. Our souls craved an entrance. We could not get enough when it happened.

Once our lips began that quest for ecstasy, then our hands, our feet, our now moistened skin slid through crevices and caves while doors and windows that previously had been locked shut were thrown open, the winds howled, and the rain pelleted. Yet, we were safe with the other, not shipwrecked at all.

When one waits five years, ten, a lifetime for this encounter, it is impossible not to cry just thinking about how long a person endures this waiting for something that is so life giving.

Much later that night, we lay still in each other's arms, our bodies still wrapped around each other's, as a perpetual cocoon.

I whispered out loud, "Life is that moment when everything you have known gets tossed overboard, and all you want to do is to reveal, to be as naked as the person who is next to you, quietly waiting for more."

There was silence then. We each pondered those words. The sun was about to rise, and faint wisps of color emerged from a darkened sky. In the distance the owls called each other, back and forth their haunting songs met. We then turned to each other, and our eyes gazed past the pupils, past the irises, past the brambles, past the skeletal remains of what had been, and we laughed and cried at the same time, not hushing our voices, not then, not ever again.

FLOATING IN CARABOSSE'S REALM

I landed in Paris a few days ago. The sky was polluted, and from the plane, the Eiffel Tower was enshrined in a thick haze. It looked quite ugly. The woman sitting next to me, who had never seen this iconic structure, kept taking picture after picture from the window. I didn't want to break her bubble and tell her that the tower looked more monstrous that day than ever.

Eiffel Tower or not, I have always been addicted to Paris. Somewhere in my brain I tell myself that all problems will miraculously go away after I go through the arduous process of getting myself on that plane and, eleven hours later, landing in this city of magical transformation.

I have visited this city many times, I have lived in this city, I have been sick in this city, I have been overwhelmed by the intensity, and I have grumbled at the unfriendliness and elitism of this city. Yet, I am eternally drawn to the endless possibilities of Paris, to the French culture, to the vast eternal brioche that gratifies famished sensory-deprived human beings such as myself.

Once I arrived, I ventured online, wondering if I might grab a ticket to the ballet, one of my greatest addictions. Of course, there was nothing available. You must book a ticket to the Paris Opera Ballet about ten years in advance. This city is nuts. But I was persistent. I went into the French web site for the ballet, and after pushing various buttons,

I discovered that there was a site for tickets that have been forfeited.

Hah!

I got into that little world, and what do you know, I found one single solitary ticket in the balcony section for a production of *"Sleeping Beauty"* for that afternoon. I struck gold. I reserved paid for it. It was mine. Mine! Mine! I floated all morning. Later that afternoon, I floated in my uncomfortable, yet beautiful shoes that didn't fit. I couldn't even walk up the stairs to my seat because I was afraid my lovely shoes would fall off and land on some person's head and I would have to explain in my imperfect French why it did this. So, I took the elevator to the top floor, found my seat, and with a smile on my face, I sat down and waited for the performance to begin.

I looked around me. There was not a seat available in the entire Opera Bastille. There were a lot of well-dressed women with well dressed, perfectly mannered daughters, and giddiness filled the air. What a happy crowd on a Sunday afternoon! And I was part of it as the lights dimmed, and the orchestra began to play, and the ornate curtain rose to a stunning entrance into a magical world.

Immediately, I immersed myself in shades of green and pink and gold, in aged archways, in tableaux that transported me to a fairy tale existence *en pointe.*

This is Paris! I said to myself, this sumptuous setting, these stunning costumes, this performance that strives towards aesthetic perfection. Nothing was left unintended. I could have stayed here forever. Probably many in the audience felt the same. My eyes became droopy. *No!* I said to myself. *Do not fall asleep!* I couldn't help it. I began to dream. Five minutes later, my eyes opened to a delicious world, a painting of greens and blues and golds.

I knew the story, expecting the spell to break. With the arrival of Carabosse, the wicked fairy, the energy changed, the music became heavy and matched the pounding of her stick on the floor, her un-leashed anger. Still, though, I was immersed in a fairy tale, and I knew the ending. Good conquers bad in fairy tales.

While the music grew in its intensity, and Carabosse flailed her body upon the stage, wreaking havoc with the sublime nature of all the fairies and their reveling, a voice emerged from the seat next to me.

"*Où est l'argent?*"

The voice was quiet, but sharp, crisp, and angry. It jolted me away from the story I was gazing at, a different kind of jolting than Carabosse's entrance. I was afraid.

"*Quoi?*" I whispered. Who was this guy? I didn't remember a man sitting next to me. I didn't look at his face. I looked down at his feet. He was wearing stiletto heels. That's what I saw when I sat down earlier. The heels. Assumptions were made.

"*Où est l'argent?*" He repeated. *Where is the money?* I thought that was what he was saying. What the hell was he talking about?

"*Vous avez dit la même chose.*" I knew my French was badly worded. I was shaking.

He pulled out a gun and pointed it at my neck.

"*Où est l'argent?*"

The gun pressed hard into my neck. I could barely breathe. I looked around me. No one seemed to have noticed. Everyone was ensconced in the wicked fairy on stage.

"*Des lumières!*" I screamed. I was shocked by the volume of my voice.

A hand was placed over my mouth.

"*Des lumières!*" I repeated in a muffled voice. I knew the word for lights, thank goodness.

The woman sitting next to me glanced at me and she saw what was going on.

"*Des lumières!*" She yelled with gusto in her voice.

Her voice was followed by a chorus of voices from the balcony.

"*Des lumières!*" Dozens of people were now yelling.

In the dark, the person with the stiletto heels rose, threw something on the ground, and then silently and unobtrusively ran away while the chorus around me engaged in screaming.

"*Des lumières!*"

At once, the curtain abruptly closed, the orchestra stopped playing and, silence filled the vast auditorium as 2700 people sat on the edge of their seats, aghast.

I looked down at the floor and saw the stiletto shoes. The gold sparkles from them twinkled and dazzled, making rainbows around me.

All eyes turned towards the balcony, when three officials approached me.

"What happened, Madame?" they asked brusquely. "This is quite an interruption. We have never experienced this, in all the years of the Paris Opera Bastille."

"There was a man who was next to me. I had never seen him before. He asked me where I put the money, and I didn't have any money, I didn't know him, and I was scared. Then he put a gun to my head and pressed it into my temple, and that's when I yelled out. He covered my mouth with his hand, and then I couldn't yell out anymore, so the audience around me, who could not see anything, began to help me by crying out for the lights!"

I was embarrassed by my accent, but still I was able to say what I needed.

"But Madame, it is not possible he had a gun. All items go through the metal detectors, so he couldn't have had a gun pressed to your temple. There are a lot of very upset patrons in this auditorium right now because of this interruption. I see there is no one in the seat next to you, and we observed no one leaving this auditorium, so on behalf of the thousands of people who are watching this program, we will be escorting you outside, and please do not return to the Opera again."

He took my arm and helped me to get up as I gathered my coat.

"But officer, there was a man, and he did press a gun to her temple. I saw it, as I was sitting right next to her."

The officer switched his gaze from me to the woman sitting next to me who spoke with a Parisian accent. He nodded his head.

He let go of my arm and sighed. He took out a notebook.

"What was he wearing, Madame?"

"Black pants, a black jacket."

"Look around. All men are wearing the same. In any case, he is gone. It is not possible he had a gun."

"He did have a gun, Monsieur." The husband of the Parisian woman, also French, spoke up.

The official looked at him seriously. "We will investigate this matter, Monsieur. Thank you for this information."

He let go of me and promptly forgot about my existence.

He put his mouth to his watch and said quietly, "Suspect with gun. Man in black pants, black jacket. Please look in all places, all men's bathrooms. Please make polite announcement for everyone to stay in their seats."

The twittering in the audience abruptly subsided as the announcement began.

"Mesdames et Messieurs, thank you for your patience while we thoroughly take care of this unfortunate interruption. We ask everyone to stay in their seats for a few moments while we conclude our investigation. Thank you very much. We will get back to you very shortly."

* * *

The house staff and the police officers scoured the halls and the men's bathrooms. One of the officers found a black plastic water gun in the toilet in one of the men's bathrooms on the 1st floor and called his colleagues over to inspect. While everyone, all the Opera Bastille staff and policemen congregated in that men's bathroom, a bare-footed figure all in black quietly crept out of the first floor women's restroom, and without being noticed quickly sped away, out the door, into the street, and into a neighboring shoe store, bought of pair of runners, and without a care, got into the subway, direction Château de Vincennes.

"This is a plastic toy gun. Of course, the metal detectors would not spot such a thing." The head officer stifled a laugh. He tried to remain serious. He would still get his paycheck, even if thousands of patrons were upset about the interruption in the performance.

He directed his mouth to his watch and stated to the official in the balcony. "All clear, everything has been resolved. Prepare to close case and resume programming."

* * *

Forty-five minutes after my first scream, the second announcement occurred.

"Mesdames et Messieurs, Thank you again for your patience and cooperation in this unfortunate interruption. The incident has been carefully resolved, and the case is closed. We will now resume our performance where we left off."

The audience heartily applauded, as the curtain rose, the orchestra resumed, and Carabosse again strutted on stage and stomped her staff across the floor. Her piercing screams echoed out into the realms of the upper balcony.

I couldn't focus on the performance though after that. An array of feelings swam through me. Anger, relief, irritation, embarrassment. Only when the French man intervened was my case justified. When the officer told me they found the gun in the men's bathroom, and they discovered it was a child's plastic water gun, I wanted to sink my head in the dirt. Then I looked at the shoes on the floor in front of me. I nodded my head and smiled. I understood. In the dark, the tops of them glittered. Quietly, I picked them up, put them in my bag, and without a sound I slipped out of the theatre, and into the metro.

There were two directions I could go on the 1 line: Château de Vincennes or La Défense. I chose the former. I needed air to breathe. I needed a forest to ground myself after my attempt to escape the world through a fairy tale.

When I arrived, the sun was streaming through the clouds. A big storm had most likely hit while I was in the theatre, the ground was wet, and puddles of water gushed through the park. It seemed like I was the only one there. I pulled out my sensible shoes from my bag, and I reveled in the idea of being a solo walker in this grand park encapsulated by the beautiful castle that adorned it.

I walked unperturbed, feeling the clicking of heels against my thigh. When the sun beamed down on my shoulders, I looked up and there was a person in front of me, staring into my eyes. He, or maybe she or maybe not he or she but some other person with some other not specified gender was gorgeous. We looked into each other's eyes, and something happened. Something not bad at all. Something electric, beautiful and unexpected occurred between us as still we stared at each other. I reached in my bag and pulled out the stilettos. We both smiled. I reached in again and pulled out a 100-euro bill. We both smiled again, and laughed, as I got closer and we touched our fingertips, and then our lips and then we pulled away after kissing for minutes, maybe hours, maybe forever as the sun beamed around us, as the fairy tale resumed.

BREAD

She never knew that a loaf of bread would save her life. But then again, she never knew that she would be in a jungle in Tanzania. She looked down at the ground, the dry, dusty earth that permeated all. The ants were at it again. They came in hordes, unannounced, hundreds of thousands of them, half of the size of her thumb, each one following the next. She watched their crawling bodies, heading away from her. They were hungry, and they seemed to be marching toward a neighbor's hut. When their bellies were empty, as was so often the case, they could consume someone's entire home in a mere two hours, their crunching sounds audible from a sizable distance. She wanted to run, to forewarn her neighbor and her family to come quickly, but when she tried to get up, she was so weak, and her body could not move. Her head spun in many directions and then stopped. Slowly she drifted into a dizzying dreamless sleep.

A week before, in the teachers' lunchroom she had heard it, alone. Every day, normally, she and all the other faculty members listened to the BBC news, reporting from London. That day, the radio, their one link to the world, had ceased its functioning and, in frustration, all the teachers had left the room. Esther had held on, hoping with a miracle that the radio would somehow find its voice. It did, minutes after her colleagues had left the room. In one singular statement, the Cambridge accent unveiled the news. Esther was sitting on the hard-back chair, listening, alone. The reality of Auschwitz was revealed. The reporter continued in a somber tone as he read the bulletin: millions so far had perished in the gas chambers.

Esther had put her head in her hands and wailed thinking of all the Jews stolen, gassed and obliterated.

* * *

No one was there to comfort her, but had the others been there, callousness would have reigned. To the other teachers, it would have been a shocking story, but it would not have affected them personally, and most likely would have funneled even more wariness toward Jews. They tolerated Esther, and even made friends with her, because of her brilliance and the fact that her students loved her, but mostly they were on her side because her husband, one of the few men in the refugee camp, fixed everything, and the women all needed him at some time. He was handsome, intelligent and kind, and the women all missed their own husbands, fighting on the front lines, oceans away. They flirted with him and ignored that he was happily married with two children and that he was, indeed, Jewish.

* * *

Before the BBC report, Esther had pondered her lecture that day, on Samuel Beckett's *Waiting for Godot*. She always loved that play and its profound simplicity, it's foreshadowing.

> *"The tears of the world are a constant quantity. For each one who begins to weep somewhere else another stops... There is man in his entirety, blaming his shoe when his foot is guilty... I'm like that. Either I forget right away, or I never forget."*

She had talked about these three lines for most of the class. She wanted her students to think about the war, to ponder what war was; she wanted them to explore the act of blame, she wanted them to feel that we are one in this world, that we all cry collectively. She wanted them to move past labels of Jewish and not Jewish, to put hatred forever aside. Most of all, she wanted them to never forget atrocities that humans assail on each other. Before listening to the truth on the radio later that day, she wanted her students to know truth in all its haunting shades. Her students at first were quiet, reserved. They were waiting for Godot, she thought out loud, for a person who would never come, for a being who would take care of them, a God, perhaps, someone. She wanted them to be that Godot, to speak up and to speak eloquently, with as much intelligence in their brains as compassion in their hearts.

They could not do it. Their silence permeated the room.

Then, the one in the back, the little blond girl, Marysia, spoke up. She had never said a word all year. Her voice wavered.

"Professor Nemirovksy, I believe you are talking about the silent Godot."

She stopped; her quiet voice became silent as Esther nodded for her to continue.

"Every time there is a pause in society, a silencing of what needs to be said, we are all silencing Godot, the figure that never comes. We are like sheep, afraid to bleat, afraid to stand up for what is not right, for injustice. We forget right away, our minds distracted. We blame others so easily, before we even look at ourselves and our silence which is made up of our hostile game. I feel the tears around the world. Look at what is happening that we, in our little jungle, are afraid to look at. Will we walk away from the awful events in the world today ignoring their credulity, or will look at our own Godots, and cry with all the rest?"

Marysia sat down, shaken by her own words. The class was quiet and stared down at their feet. Esther stood, her hands on her hips, and shook her head. She smiled and shook her head again, amazed at her student's brilliance, her insights pouring out of that small being, the fire in her belly that inspired life.

She loved teaching, those moments when it is not about the teacher, but when the students, their minds, their hearts, splay open; when they get it, and they leap. They dive into a lake. They are tentative at first, their arms outstretched, and then they do it, following the curve of the body, the line of a perfect arc into the water.

Teaching had taken her away from the world, even if she had been instructing her students to be a part of it.

After Marysia spoke there was a rumble in the classroom. There was no escaping the wisdom that had just emerged. A window had been opened. Silence prevailed for a few moments until Irinia, a robust teenager, muscles emanating from her thighs, stood.

"We were not raised to think this way, Professor Nemirovsky. We were told to be complacent and look at us. We are displaced from our country, our homes were stolen away from us, now housing the Nazis. Our fathers are dying on the front lines, and there *is* no Godot. We are not waiting for a ghost that will never arrive. We were taught to hate, to judge, to take for ourselves. When our fathers are gone, and we are stuck with our mothers to raise us, what will we know then? Where will we go after this? My little sister barely remembers Poland. All she knows is our grass huts and the banana trees that one day she longs to climb. We were told to be complacent, but I see a better world, one where we have the power to not wait for what does not make sense."

Esther stood, her petite body illuminated in the sun that poured through the window, again nodded her head, wanting more.

Bronek, in the back, raised his hand. Esther nodded to him to speak.

"We were taught to hate Jews," he began, stirring up the class, their heads fixed on his. "I know what is happening over there in Europe. They think we're dummies, like we are not supposed to know the truth. They are killing them, hundreds of thousands, maybe even millions of Jews, slaughtering them, rounding them up and thinking this is the final solution to making a better world. They think we are supposed to believe this. Then they, like you read to us, tell us to blame our shoes when our feet are guilty. Then they run away, smiling. It is disgusting, this world is disgusting, the lies are disgusting. We are taught that we must hate. If I were German, I would be killing people right now. I would be part of the Hitler Juden, the young who are forced into a world of propagating hatred, and I wouldn't have a choice. Thank God, I am Polish, and I am here, but what good is it to be safe, to be a refugee, when the world around me is threatened, is perishing, at the mercy of one man who has deemed this? We came here, all of us, quiet and meek, scared and squirming. Now, we are different. We have all changed, we have come of age in Tanganyika, and we have you as the most influential teacher we have ever had and most probably ever will have."

With that pronouncement, he sat down and folded his hands. The bell rang, and it was time for lunch. One by one the students filed out, looking down. They seemed afraid to show Esther how they felt about what had transpired in class that day. When the room was silent, and she was alone with the echo of the words that had just been spoken, she began to shake, her heart raw with emotions that overtook her. She looked at the now empty chairs that sat in rows facing her, the energy still in the wood reflecting those minds that housed compassion, that screamed out for change in the blighted world.

* * *

Esther put her head in her hands and wailed. She was alone in the teacher's lunchroom. Her class, the discussion, the philosophy of mankind were the last things on her mind now. *Millions of Jews gassed, they reported. Philosophy will never explain this. My father, my brother, my grandparents, my in-laws, my cousins, my aunts, and uncles. Gone. Why me?*

Her mind raced, the guilt of survival overcame all the facts and figures that had been reported. While the midday heat smothered life around her, she shuddered in her hands, feeling her breath, her vile breath against her skin.

I should be there with them, perishing together, why did I escape?

She forgot then about her husband, her two children. Nothing mattered anymore as she trudged back home to her empty hut. With no more classes to teach that day, she went to her mattress on the packed earthen floor and cried. She never cried. Her tears felt foreign, and she didn't know what to think. She felt scared.

She could not imagine living anymore. Hearing the truth, knowing it now, made her sick. Life was nothing. Her family, and millions of others, were gone, incinerated. She fell asleep, a restless sleep until her husband and children came home. Then, she slept harder, and they could not wake her. In the morning, when she still had not woken up, her husband called the doctor. He diagnosed her with the flu and prescribed sleep. When the family had left for work and school, she opened her eyes and lay motionless in her bed. She rolled over, feeling hunger pains.

Now, all is different. I no longer wish to call myself a survivor.

She felt her throat close as she envisioned her brother, her beloved brother, gassed, his own breath suffocated, his sweet laughter stolen forever. She had a vision of him the last time she saw him, when her youngest daughter was just born. He was so happy holding his little niece in his strong arms. He whispered something in her ear. She always wondered what he had said.

Esther rolled over, feeling the hunger pains invade her brain. Now, all was different. She began to moan. Hunger mixed with a haunting mournful wail for all the dead, for all the corpses laid out in her mind's eye. She stared at the door of the hut and her vision, distorted, saw ants, millions of them, troops on the front lines heading towards her, approaching fast and faster. Her breathing became rapid, and then in her distorted state her brother appeared, and he stomped them out with his big, thick boots. He wore a Star of David around his neck, and he laughed and laughed. His laughter lingered and echoed throughout the camp. He lifted his sister up in his arms, still laughing as they fled the camp, running through the savannah and away, her dress flying in the air.

I must be dying, she thought. *It is time.* She felt her skin, how it had lost its softness, dry and brittle now, parched and without fluid. She could barely open her mouth; her lips were cracked and starved. She closed her eyes, waited and groaned.

Her mind drifted to the day the Russians had taken them away, in the middle of the night. She remembered the trains, hard, rough wood. All around her was vomit and excrement, and no one knew where they were going. *Hell,* she thought. *I have left heaven and now I am heading to hell,* she had said to herself.

One week later, they had arrived in Siberia, at a forced labor camp, where barbed wire surrounded them with a metal vice. Stalin was saving the Poles, they had been told. She wanted to spit in Stalin's face as she was forced to haul lumber. In her younger life, she had worked and toiled, studied and had confronted poverty. She had met every kind of obstacle to become the first woman at her university to be granted a

Ph. D. And Stalin was saving her now? She was starving in Siberia, and she could barely wake up each day.

Her once healthy children quickly lost weight, became sick and emaciated. Her oldest had to learn Russian and sold Esther's lingerie in the black market so that she could get another loaf of stale bread for the family that week.

Lying in bed, her thoughts turned to their eventual escape from Siberia, being promised refugee status in a British camp in East Africa. They thought they were lucky. War had warped their minds, and now what was lucky was survival. Her husband almost died from typhus in the middle of Uzbekistan, where no doctors would treat Jews. She had managed to find a Jewish doctor, hidden in the folds of the earth, who gave him seven pills, and again, survival had licked their lips. Weeks later, they were in a bus, on a mountainside in Iran. The brakes failed, and had it not been for a tree that caught that bus, again, death could have climbed in. In Tanganyika, their neighbor's home was eaten by ants. Somehow, theirs was left untouched.

Hitler brought me to this place.

Her thoughts turned to that man, and she convulsed, her body wracked with the poison of his being. She could not push him away. She tried to get him out of her thoughts, but still he prevailed, his insidious smile curved at the corners, spewing fire out of his eyes.

Esther tried to turn over in her bed. She tried to rid his image away from torturing her, but she could not move. She tried to scream, but nothing came out but her own gagged silence.

* * *

Later that afternoon, as the sun waned and the trees swayed gently with the first of the evening breeze, she heard something.

There were incessant knocks on the door.

She tried to ignore them.

They became louder and sounded like bullets to her head. She groaned. Her hunger had turned her into something primitive.

Footsteps approached her. Her cloudy vision could see only vague forms. She could not speak.

Their faces drawn and worried, her students held it to her nose. A fresh loaf of bread they had just made. They had spent all day at it, missed their classes, fumbled with the recipe and had stolen ingredients from the camp kitchen. They had watched their mothers make bread in Poland, and they tried to make a loaf from the old ways, using their elbows to check for the correct oven temperature.

Esther thought they were apparitions and continued her moaning. The students didn't leave, they waved the freshly baked bread under her nose and watched the steam rise, the flavors of the rye and the wheat mixing with the yeast, wafting through the air.

Esther ceased her guttural sounds and became silent. Her nose twitched. The scent of the bread filled it.

Her mouth instinctively opened.

Her students excitedly tore off a small piece and gently placed it on their teacher's tongue.

Her mouth closed. The crumb dissolved. Again, she opened her mouth, and the students broke off a slightly larger piece of bread and placed it into the awaiting vessel of life.

As the sun drifted behind the trees, creating shadows and a darkened room, the students continued. Her mouth opened, their beloved professor's mouth, and they, the adoring students, fed her, bite by bite.

They watched her, moment by moment, return to life.

She first regained vision. From the smells to the tastes, now she could see what it was she was eating. Bread, the staff of life, began to wake her, and connected her to a force inside herself that went beyond guilt, grief and beyond the agony of what humans do to each other, to a place that chooses survival once again.

She opened her eyes and managed to smile.

"We almost lost you, dear Professor," Marysia said. Her dark eyes pierced the small space.

"Why did you want to leave us?" Bronek asked.

"I didn't want to leave you. I didn't want to leave anyone. It's just sometimes the world is so ugly." She looked into their hopeful eyes. She often wondered who needed whom more.

Maybe at the end of the day, teaching is all about feeding hungry mouths and being fed back.

She took one last big bite of bread and savored each morsel. The doughy piece slid down into her almost satiated belly.

She rose and her students took her by the hand and watched her feet touch the earth.

"Please, don't tell my family."

Her students nodded. It would be their secret that they saved the life of their beloved teacher.

They took her by the hand and led her outside. It was early evening. Sitting on the ground surrounded by banana trees, waiting for her, her husband and her two daughters ran to Esther and put their arms around her. In the distance, frogs and crickets and owls made a chorus, and even farther away, wild dogs echoed their voices into a screeching song, as the blooming Datura flowers around them spread their intoxicating nightly scents.

Survival was everywhere, the pulsing and constantly moving and changing motions of living beings. Esther smiled, while she broke off pieces of freshly baked bread and gave them to her family, looking in their eyes as they ate, remembering the day she got married, the moments her children were born. All her memories came to her as they devoured that bread, and they laughed into the night, while the warm breezes accompanied them, the chorus of animals continued and the sky around them was blazoned with stars, light and darkness enveloping all.

CANNING

She asked me to can plums with her. This would be the first time she wanted me to share her usual solitary midsummer ritual. I wondered: "Why this year?" But I quickly dismissed these thoughts, relishing my position as "the chosen one."

Ever since Dziadzia, my grandfather, died fifteen years earlier, picking Baba's Santa Rosa plums had been my job. Every July I would climb the old, gnarled tree. With one hand hanging onto a limb, I would shake the intricately formed branches with the other hand and watch the ripe plums tumble to the ground. Then, I would scramble in the thick ivy below and collect at least two aromatic and juicy bags full of summer's sweetness.

Then, I would proudly present my harvest to Baba, who would, each time, smile and remark with her thick Polish accent, "Ah! What am I to do with all these plums! So many plums!" She would, though, every year, can all alone the best plums for our winter dinners at her house. We never really liked those canned plums, however. They did not have enough sugar in them, and they no longer tasted like summer. We had to close our eyes while eating them because they were so tart. Yet, they were Baba's canned plums, from her tree, picked and preserved in the prime of those Berkeley Hills' summers where there was usually more fog than sun.

In 1991 Baba was already old and had been for some time. She would be ninety that October. I loved her oldness, such wisdom she had, such beauty in every wrinkle, bent joint, and in her hunched back. She was a little over four feet tall by then. I sensed that each wrinkle, fold, and imperfection housed a story, and often more than one. A Holocaust survivor with a Ph. D. in German Literature from the Jagiellonian University in Krakow, Poland, Baba had many harrowing stories to tell. During that summer of 1991, they seemed to carry even more weight than in previous years. I had heard these stories for much of my childhood and young adulthood, but when she approached nine-ty, she began to tell them to me with greater emotional intensity than ever. I became her confidante for much of this emotional content. As a devout intellectual, Baba usually kept her feelings hidden deep inside, and this transformation represented a significant change for her and for our relationship. I would listen for hours to her stories and the trauma she experienced. Then, when it was time to say goodbye for the evening, I would kneel to her level, rest my head on her shoulder, and she would hug me.

That July marked the culmination of this deep bonding between grandmother and granddaughter. The plums became our medium. That day I performed my usual collecting task. The harvest was more bountiful than any other year. Baba briefly explained the canning pro-cedure: a little water here, a little sugar there. She seemed to pride herself on her vagueness and improvisation while it was clear she had command of her creations in her kitchen. After we haphazardly per-formed the basic preparations, we stood side by side in silence, and packed plums into the awaiting jars. To me, this silence between us spoke lessons of a lifetime, a shared culture, our Jewish heritage; there was in that room a sense of awe that was being passed down through three generations. The red juice bathed our hands and our arms, and seemed akin to the pain and suffering, as well as the hope and determination that so much epitomized Baba's life.

She admired the way I packed the plums in the jars and complained that hers were too awkwardly placed. We both laughed at our clumsiness and at the delicious mess we were making. After we fit the caps on the jars and put them in the big pot to boil, we each cried. These shared tears celebrated our accomplishment, our joy in being together to preserve this ritual. I think, though, that one of us also had tears of mourning of an impending loss.

* * *

Just a little over a month later, in August, Baba asked me if I would help her can several bags of peaches that she had bought on sale at Safeway. There was, this time, a slight urgency in her voice that I only detected much later. This message, "Would you help me?" revealed itself as we approached the day: now, she needed me to continue her yearly peach canning. Because of this fervent need, the canning of the peaches took on, from the start, a very different flavor from the ritual that belonged to the plums just weeks before.

My parents had just returned from a long-awaited vacation to the British Isles, a trip they had postponed for a few years because of my father's stroke. Baba had worried about that trip for months. She claimed that her worries grew out of her fear for her son-in-law's health on such a long trip, but I sensed this was only part of it. Baba became quite depressed while they were gone. Her smiles vanished. During those few weeks we noticed her very being had begun to slip through the cracks in her walls. She spoke to me of this depression, and while I listened and later helped her laugh some of it off, I sensed in her a gnawing pain. She seemed entrapped in fear and dread. How alone she must have felt. She never discussed death with us, but I felt it creep around her with greater intensity.

She seemed to need family more than usual. She seemed to need ritual. But I also knew she hated this feeling of distress. She was a woman who conquered, not submitted. I could tell that she was overwhelmed by the many bags of peaches we were to can, peaches that required skinning and slicing, where the plums did not. Baba was exceptionally tired that afternoon. The ritual seemed way too arduous, yet I could tell it was important for her to do it. I did all the preparation work this time. She joined me as we put the sliced peaches inside our jars. Again, we stood in silence, yet this time our silence was weighed down with sadness that neither of us could label, nor even really know the full extent of. I felt Baba's tiredness. I felt exhausted too.

The yellowish red juice slid down our arms. It felt like a jaundiced poison that marred what could have been a celebration of mid-summer, bottled up and preserved in glass jars. After the peaches made it to the cooking stage, Baba nearly collapsed in her chair. She instructed me to finish the rest. I floundered, burned myself, screamed and cried in her kitchen. I felt confused, sad, and angry. I felt abandoned by my companion, teacher, and my mentor. My grandmother was slipping away from me in a quiet exhaustion. I couldn't finish those peaches alone. I realized then that I could not be that "chosen one" to continue her sacred traditions. I needed her.

During my tantrum, my father appeared at the door. He had arrived to fix a leaking faucet. When he saw my tears, the troubled peaches and his mother-in-law looking very tired in her kitchen, he calmly put on an apron. He told us he had never canned fruit, but had, as a boy, watched his mother every year preserve the summertime's offerings.

With few words between us, he and I worked side by side. I felt his gentle support in harmony with Baba's grateful sighs.

After he left, when I said goodbye to my grandmother that evening, she told me repeatedly how she wished she could have been there for me throughout the canning process. She felt so guilty for her dependence on others. Yet, as I put my head on her shoulder and felt her arms around me, like I always did, I sensed her great relief that together, we had preserved an important ritual. Maybe she realized that to allow a tradition to be passed down, she would need to let go of those parts she could not do. Maybe, too, she realized she would need to let go of the tradition itself, trusting that it would be caught, embraced, and carried on by that "chosen one." Baba, reluctantly did let go, and I, reluctantly, caught the threads.

* * *

Autumn came quickly that year. The air was colder than usual. In the middle of October Baba received from a friend several bags of Lake County pears. Canning those pears seemed impossible for her. Her summertime question "Would you help me?" turned into, "Would you do them for me?" that fall. Gone this time was any desire to preserve these fruits. For her now, they simply needed to be done.

Baba and I had just celebrated our joint birthdays with the family. My grandmother had turned ninety that year, an age she never expected to reach, and that for years had talked of with tones of dread. On the 8th of October, everyone gathered at her house, sat around the well-used teak oval dinner table and ate a delicious meal my mother had made. We ended the feast with our usual two birthday cakes. Baba and I sat side by side, connected by blood, by moons, and by our birthday. Her annual toast was different that year. Her words were barely audible through tears that seemed to come from a primal place. Perhaps they were tears of joy, celebrating once again the two birthdays and the whole family together. But more likely it seemed like they were tears of desperate sadness and pain. Without saying it, our Baba was signaling to her family, to the ones she loved best, that she was dying. I held her hand tighter that evening than ever. I could not stop hugging her and wanting her close to me. While she tried to reciprocate my affection, as she always used to, especially on our birthdays, that night she rested in another place, a place inaccessible to all of us. Underneath our laughter, our birthday joy, our celebration of family and matriarchy, we all knew that this would be our last family reunion with Baba.

Exactly one week before she died, on the 4th of November, I arrived at her house, ready, yet never ready to can her pears. Pears have always been for me the epitome of an autumn fruit, representing a season of transition from the sun-filled carefree days of spring and summer to the introspective, serious, and death-infused weeks of late autumn and winter. Baba always hated this time of year, hated feeling cold and homebound. Sitting at the kitchen table next to her little space heater comforted her, yet the cold of the old house whipped around every other room and overwhelmed her.

That afternoon, Baba remained mostly in her other place and let me carry on by myself with the pears. I didn't really know what I was doing, and I didn't really care. I stood at the counter, in silence and alone, and worked away at the ominous pears. I hated the clear, color-less liquid that ran down my arms. It was the same color as the angry tears that welled up inside me that I dared this time not come out. I worked quickly, wanting to get the job done so I could return to Baba, who sat at the table and stared off into her distant world.

Finally finished, I sat down to a warmed-up dinner prepared by my mother earlier in the week. While we ate, Baba once again talked about her depression. But this time, she told me solemnly and perhaps secretly that she felt ready to go. I put my fork down and went over to her. I bent down low and put my head on her very weak shoulder. I couldn't stop crying.

"Baba," I said through my tears, "No matter what state you are in, no matter where you are, I want you to know that I will always love you."

We cried together. We both knew that this would be our last time together. The rest of the evening we were mostly silent. I washed the dishes, laid the pears to rest, promised her I would see her soon, like I always did, even if I knew I never would.

* * *

One year later, the many jars of plums, peaches, and pears that we canned together sat untouched on Baba's basement shelves.

The following summer and fall, though, as if by instinct, I began my own process of canning. In July, I stood in her plum tree, shook its delicate branches and watched the juicy plums fall to the ground. I collected them in my paper bag smiling and crying while I said out loud to our tree: "Ah yes, there will always be plums, so many plums."

WAVES IN BLUE

The back of my car is full of her clothes, mostly fine silks and wool, all purchased in this country. Nothing of the old world remains. Those were probably burned, or maybe they were given to the wives of the SS. I take a whiff, smelling her, and the sweetness invades my nostrils with her perfumes, her imported soaps from Spain. I imagine her celebrating freedom from the brutish existence that was once hers. I imagine her dancing in the streets of America.

Soon after my grandmother died in early November 1991, my mother, heeding the words from her mother's will, asked me to donate all her clothes to the Jewish Home for the Aged in San Francisco. I do not want to go but feel I need to do what my grandmother requested.

I am at the approach to the Golden Gate Bridge on Highway 101. The clouds are thick and heavy. It is late November, and I feel chilled from the wind gusts. One of the windows in my car does not close all the way. On an impulse, I take a detour, quickly veering off the highway, away from San Francisco, away from the Bridge, and I go on the small road towards the Marin Headlands. I drive down my favorite Conzelman Road, the one that abruptly descends and gives way to a panoramic expanse of the Pacific Ocean. At the end of the road is Rodeo Beach. The sky is huge and dark, and the waves are high and ominous.

I feel swallowed up in the immensity of it all. I begin to cry. Something primitive in me gets activated, and I do not know what is really happening, except I have a sense that I am about to do something that will be life changing. No one is around; I am alone. I park my car at the beach parking lot, open the back door and pick up my grandmother's blue dress from the top of the pile of clothes on the seat. It's more than a dress, though. It is a royal blue wool dress with a matching tunic. She wore it on special occasions, and often with a simple gold necklace. I always thought she looked like a queen in it, someone regal, filled with knowledge, a presence that commanded respect and admiration. Someone who survived. I take the blue outfit, and I walk towards the beach, the pounding waves. I notice a small thread is dangling from the bottom seam. I break it off with my teeth and put it in my pocket. Then, I heave the dress and the tunic into the wildly oncoming tide, and I watch the blue get swallowed up by the merciless waters.

I gasp.

Gone. The blue dress is gone. I bite my lip and taste blood. I get back in my car, drive through the headlands, to the approach of the Bridge, and I merge into the speeding oncoming traffic. I arrive at the other side of the ocean, the other side of the bridge.

I am in San Francisco.

"Fuck! What did I do? The blue dress is gone!" I scream out loud; the cars around me honk like maimed geese.

I make a suicidal U turn, and head back over the bridge, back to the beach. I want it back, that dress, I want her back, my grandmother. Neither appear. It is dark now. The tide is higher than ever, spewing out the remains of a meal, preparing itself for the biggest storm of the season.

* * *

The journey of this dress will depend on many factors. Waves, water, tides, microorganisms. Wool decomposes easily. Because of this, the dress will probably not travel far, will never reach The North Pacific Gyre. It will not be washed up on some beach across the world. Most likely it will sink to the bottom of the ocean, since wool gets very heavy when it is wet. Probably within a few months, the wool fibers will swell up, the blue dye will vanish, and marine microscopic animals will eat up the keratin protein found in many kinds of wool.

* * *

I drive home that day and, on my bed, I cry. I feel so stupid. Why didn't I keep the dress? I loved that dress. If it reminded me of my grandmother, why did I even put it in my car? Why did I throw it in the ocean? That was such an inane thing to do. What was I thinking? Did I want to erase the dress from my mind…or did I want to keep it?

* * *

Carmel, California, a small seaside town one hundred miles or so south of San Francisco, held, every spring, a Coastal Clean Up Day. On the eighteenth of April 1992, dozens of well-minded citizens of this progressive community gathered under a dazzlingly beautiful spring sky to clean any washed-up trash from their usual pristine beaches. Everyone was happy. It had been an extremely cold and wet winter on the Central California coast, and the prospect of a sweet spring day was tantalizing.

The rules were simple: wear gloves, take a garbage bag, and collect anything you can find that is not organic. There would be a prize for the most original piece of trash.

Lucie, a Czech-born former hippie and retired high school art teacher at Carmel High, strolled down the beach with her dog, Mathilda. Lucie was known throughout the small town as the eccentric one, the one who had carved out for herself a bucolic life of creativity and imagination. She lived in a tree house, of sorts, a small cabin perched on the bluff of the Pacific Ocean, surrounded by Monterey Pines. She prided herself on being a steward of the earth and ocean and made it her calling to clean up any garbage she could find on the beaches that she regularly walked on. Naturally, it made sense she would attend the town's annual Coastal Clean-up Day. She waved at all the locals when she arrived, happy that everyone was out doing what she did anyway every week. Everyone waved back, smiling. There wasn't a soul in Carmel who did not like Lucie and her sweet, gentle Shetland sheep dog, Mathilda. Some of Lucie's former students were there that morning and greeted her. They didn't linger, however. They seemed resolutely invested in winning the prize and in finding the most original piece of trash.

Lucie followed Mathilda, whose nose was, as usual, glued to the ground, always looking for organic material to roll around in. The dog ventured further down the beach, away from the crowds. They both had their noses glued to the sand, looking for different things, but their common denominator was looking. Time was inconsequential, and it was such a beautiful day, with the gentle spring sun warming their bodies, they both strolled even farther down the beach, towards Big Sur. It was a negative low tide, and everything alive was out, it seemed, enjoying this day, crawling around. Mathilda was overjoyed and found her calling in tide pool after tide pool.

Lucie smiled. She noticed that there seemed to be a blueish tinge to the water, in one of the tide pools that her dog was joyfully pawing through. It struck her as odd, because blue was not a normal color on the beach. She looked closely and noticed something coming out of the sand. It was a piece of fabric, or so it seemed, that was of a brilliant shade of blue, more like a royal blue. It was mostly buried in the sand, and only a bit of it stuck out that she could see. Always on her beach walks she carried a small shovel with her for these purposes. She began to dig and dig and gradually was able to uncover what appeared to be the sleeve of a woman's dress. She was so excited, she continued for several minutes and finally pulled out a long-sleeved very soggy wool dress with a matching tunic. A rusty safety pin connected the two pieces.

* * *

I try not to think too much about that day, the beach, the dress. I try not to think too much about my grandmother. It's easier that way, I find, to put aside things that are painful, a person I was attached to who is no longer here. A decade somehow passes. In those ten years, I got married, and subsequently, got divorced. My life, admittedly, is somewhat of a blur.

In 2002, however, at the beginning of a new millennium, something happened to me. I think it is time for something different, but I am not sure what. I buy my first computer, and I spend hours surfing the web.

In late September that year, I type Jewish feminists in the search bar of my desktop. I don't know why I requested this information. I feel like some part of me wanted to know something on this topic, but I don't know where this feeling comes from. My grandmother was somewhat of a Jewish feminist. Maybe that was why I started this search. Hmmm… Anyway, a plethora of information comes up, but what catches my eye is a Jewish feminist Tashlich event. I realize it is

Rosh Hashonah, an important holiday that my grandmother honored every year. The Rosh Hashanah ritual that is listed is to be held that Saturday at the beach at Steep Ravine at the foot of Mount Tamalpais, off Highway 1, north of San Francisco. Attendees are asked to bring a small shovel and something biodegradable to toss into the waves. Swimsuits or some other attire that can get wet are suggested; a towel is, too. Nudity is acceptable, the listing states.

* * *

Lucie Cermak greets everyone with a huge smile. She is an older woman, about eighty I think, with grey braids that she ties with purple ribbons. Her face is soft, welcoming. I love her smile. She makes me feel happy. I smile back and realize I have not been smiling much lately. It hurts my face, actually; muscles I don't use anymore.

It is a perfect late afternoon. The autumn sun is gentle slowly going down, and there is a light breeze. There are eight of us, women of all sizes and shapes. I am the smallest one. Everyone is chatting while we follow Lucie from the parking lot at the top of the hill to the beach. The ocean goes on forever, to the right and the left of us.

"Welcome to one of my favorite places in the world!" Lucie says, beaming.

She leads us to a secluded section of the beach. She then instructs us to remove our shoes, and any article of clothing we don't want to get wet, and to take our shovels with us. Some women take everything off and are naked. I have on an old swimsuit, something I have had since the 1980's. Lucie takes off all her clothes and keeps on a long-sleeved sweater. We put our clothes carefully in a separate pile at the top of the beach. The tide is way out. It appears to be a super negative low tide. The sand is wet and oozes between my toes. There are boulders around us, and the beach seems like a private nook. No one is around except us. I smell sulfur.

Lucie tells us that when it is an exceptionally negative low tide, you can dig out a natural hot spring, which is what we will be doing. We excitedly begin to dig the sand with our shovels and our hands, making a deep pit for us to stand in. The water is warm, a perfect temperature, and the setting sun creates an orange glow in the sky. We are all chatting as we work. Lucie laughs and tells us that this is sort of like when she dug out a dress, ten years earlier, buried in the sand in Carmel.

"You dug out a dress?" One of the women asks.

"Yes!" she responds, smiling. "I think it must have been washed up in the tide."

I look at her and stare.

"What did it look like? What shape was it in?" another woman asks.

"It was in perfect condition, a royal blue very elegant woolen dress with a tunic attached with a safety pin. It was incredibly heavy, very waterlogged, though, and I had to wring it out several times, and then I dragged it to my car, and took it to the cleaners in town."

I stare harder.

"Do you ever wear it?" another woman asks.

"All the time. Every year on my birthday. I call it my "birthday suit."

Everyone laughs. I can't stop staring at her.

She looks at me and smiles. I wonder if she knows I know.

She changes the subject and tells us we can use the milk crates someone has left on the beach, and we place those at the bottom of the pit we have just made, to sit on later if we want. She then instructs us to get out for a moment, take the object that we have brought that we want to release, and then, return to the hot spring and we will begin our Tashlich ritual.

I am shaking while I walk over to my pants and take from my pocket what I had brought.

When we return to the pit, I notice that Lucie has taken off her sweater and is now naked. She has a beautiful, round body, full of wrinkles. I glance again and notice she has six numbers tattooed on her forearm.

I gulp. I quickly do the math. She was about twenty when she got out.

* * *

She asks us to close our eyes. She calls out the four directions: North, South, East, and West. She suggests we call the ancestors to our circle if we want. She asks us to breathe in the beauty in front of us, and to breathe out and let go of anything in our bodies, our minds, our relationships, or even the world that is troubling us.

Then she asks us to open our eyes, while still being in our quiet selves and in our process of Tashlich.

"Tashlich," she says in a gentle tone, "is about release." She pauses and looks up at the sky that is still wild with color.

"We release what is important to us in the water, because water is a vehicle for movement and transformation. We release what is in our pockets, because symbolically our pockets are what is close to our bodies and our psyches. We release, and thereby let go of what, in this past year, we are no longer needing. This could be a story we have held on to, a pattern of behavior, a way of living, a relationship to a person or even an idea, anything really. There is no prescription for Tashlich. It is completely subjective, what is meaningful to you. When you release, you create space in your psyche for newness, and that is what the new year is about."

She pauses and looks at each of us. She smiles.

"Each of you has something in your hand that came from your pockets. One by one, when you feel the time is right, I want you to step out of this little protected cave we have made, take your object and walk down to the surf. Throw your object into the waves. Say a prayer, say whatever you want out loud or to yourself with the intent to let go of that which is troubling you. If you wish, you may come back to our hot spring after you are done, or you may stay along the waves. Whatever feels right."

The first woman to do her Tashlich is the largest one in the group. She gets up and walks to the waves. She is quiet and then, when she heaves what is in her hand, she roars. Her wail echoes along the beach. Then she quietly returns to the hot spring, closes her eyes and smiles.

I am next, the smallest one after the largest one. I get up. I do not show Lucie what is in my hand. She will never know. I go to the water, I open my tightly balled fist, and I gently let go of the fine royal blue thread that I have kept in my jewelry box for the last ten years. I begin to cry and I cannot stop. I remember that fateful day so vividly. I remember imagining what it might be like to have put on that dress, to look in the mirror, to smell her elegance, to merge with my grandmother, history meeting the present. She was the survivor. She was, in that dress, like a swan, with swirling masses of horror lurking from her past. Yet, she stood, with the gold around her neck, saying every year at Passover, "Wasn't it enough that we survived the atrocities that we did?"

I am crying even harder, feeling the waves around my feet. I feel my hands. They have always been soft, so fragile. I feel like I am a remnant of her story, that piece of history that does not make sense, that jars the mind, a pain that does not get erased.

My tears begin to subside. When I threw the dress into the sea, it did not and never will erase the dress. The tide goes in, and it goes out, yet it is the particles that get left behind. Those are the ones that matter. Those are the ones I can lodge in my memory, making me who I am, a decade later, after the last breath of my grandmother, the last dazzling blue threads smoothed out by the constant motion of the waves.

I am no longer crying. Survival is this. Somehow, from devastation, abundance evolves. It's like a return to life, or in French, a *renaissance*, beyond a dress in cold water, beyond a memory of someone I adored who is now gone. Maybe it's like that feeling of waking up after a good night's sleep, after a decade of sleeping poorly. Ahhh, the possibilities of finally sleeping well.

I am ready to leave the surf, but one more thing comes to mind: my grandmother's favorite play to teach to her students was *Waiting for Godot*. The irony was that she never did wait for the hero that never comes. She was and she became her own hero. I want to think of that image and hold onto it, as if there is a camera that is fixed on one spot, the face, for example, with the light just so, as the curtain closes and then goes up again for the next act.

I am finished with my Tashlich. I walk back to the hot spring and gently sink my whole body into the warm, fragrant water. I feel a smile spread across my face. I strip off my swimsuit and let everything I had just done, everything that is now new to me, plunge into my soul.

ACKNOWLEDGMENTS

First of all, my infinite thanks to my editor and ally, Aude Ramadier, who consistently knows how to take every word, every comma, every nuance I write and make them all fit somehow into what seems like a perfect circle. I don't know how she does it.

The creation of a short story is, I like to think, like the creation of a glimpse of time, a fragment of a life that you can hold in your hand, a manageable piece of humanity that can escape the realm of the overwhelming agenda that so often plagues us. I know many people who cannot read novels for that reason but instead find solace in a short story. This genre of writing is, in many ways, a balm in a shattered world, a means of escape that is tangible, does not linger, and, like a bee or a butterfly, lets you sit in the flower, absorbing as much nectar as possible before it is time to move to the next flower.

These eighteen short stories, written over the course of the last three and a half decades, are the result of my work on the art of observation, something that I was not so good at in my younger years. Each story is based on some historical fact, someone I have known, or none of the above. In the latter case, it is my imagination gone wild.

In "The Red Dress", for example, Yehudi Menuhin did indeed play his violin at Bergen-Belsen Concentration camp the day the prisoners were freed. He was interviewed on the radio several years ago. I was so moved by his words and knew I had to write a story.

And in "Forty Shades of Life," the Hide-and-Seek Children indeed existed: Holocaust survivor children from Slovakia were brought to

Clonyn Castle in Ireland to recover; a monumental project that was organized by Rabbi Dr. Solomon Schonfeld.

If you happened to read my previous book, *From the Outside*, you might recognize similarities between it and the short story "Bread", from this collection. No, your mind is not deceiving you. Indeed, "Bread" came first, and I liked the story so much, that I put parts of it into sections of *From the Outside*. Sometimes in life, when you land on something you like, it is worth repeating, don't you think?

In many of these stories, someone I knew well, or perhaps only met once, gave me the inspiration to write a story about their story. People's lives are brilliant, beautiful, often tragic, and seemingly hopeless. But, underneath the insidious layers, hope prevails, going beyond courage to a place of love, where survival is met with a light that emerges from within. At least that is what I see, and I love to express this in my writing.

Thank you to all those people who have inspired these stories.

Thank you to my nibling Iz Ullmann who provided me with thoughtful insight regarding the ritual of Tashlich.

Thank you to my two sisters, Vicki and Diane, who read these stories carefully and offered their astute commentary.

Thank you to Sharon Blyth-Moss for creating, once again, a stunning book cover that wowed me from the moment she showed me her work.

And thank you always to Gorham Printing and Kathy Campbell, who appear at the end of the book making process and weave their magic.

ABOUT THE AUTHOR

Heidi Harrison, author of *The Four Seasons* (Sapphire Books Publishing), *When Paris Was Her Lover* (Emerald House Publishing), and *From the Outside* (Emerald House Publishing), has always loved writing. At a very early age, she realized that words allowed for the exodus of her soul, a rhapsody, a sense of grace enveloping her. Writing has been her boulder, her stories the healing balm in a world that sometimes cries out for this. She was born and raised in the San Francisco Bay Area. She holds a MS degree in Counseling Psychology, and a dual degree in Child Development and French, and she spent almost thirty years as a psycho-therapist and a teacher of young children. She is also a classically trained violinist. She has traveled extensively between the hemispheres and has lived and studied in Paris and in Grenoble, France. She has written several novels and children's books, countless stories, (fiction and creative nonfiction) and a full-length memoir. In each of these works, she is inspired by imagination itself, by real stories of people's lives, by love, by music, by the stunning majesty of nature, by the beauty and power of words, relationships, the diversity of cultures, and the resilience of the human heart. We live in a complicated and often challenging world, and yet, as a writer, an observer, and as a teacher, she is, every day, inspired by the grace and by the infinite beauty that we, as humans, embody. Our dazzling earth is of an infinite nature; humbly, she lets words only begin to describe it.

Website: www.heidimharrison.com

Facebook: https://www.facebook.com/HeidiEmeraldHarrison.Author/

Praise for Heidi's previous book, *From the Outside:*
A powerful, unforgettable read from the heart

I've been sitting with *From the Outside* for months now—honestly, it's one of those books that lingers, the kind that quietly follows you into your day-to-day long after you've put it down. Maybe it hit me even harder because I know Heidi, and I know how much of her own soul she poured into this story. But even without that, this book is extraordinary.

From the Outside isn't just historical fiction—it's emotional archaeology. It's a journey through time and memory and body, a tender, raw exploration of inherited trauma and identity. Helen's story—her questioning, her vulnerability, her aching need to understand what's been passed down to her—is both deeply personal and universally resonant, especially for those of us who are children (or grandchildren) of survivors.

I found myself holding my breath through passages about Helen's mother, Ewa—the stoic, shining version of the American dream overlaying the quiet, buried horror of what she endured. The way Heidi unspools that trauma—not through spectacle, but through silence, nuance, and what *isn't* said—masterful. I was especially struck by how the book illustrates that trauma doesn't end with survival. It carries on, lives in the body, the bloodline. You feel it in Helen's physical illness, in her confusion, her grief for people she never met but somehow still mourns.

There's a vividness to the writing that made the suffering of this family — through Siberia, through the refugee camps in Africa—feel immediate and tangible. The roll of the dice, the wafer-thin chance between life and death, the sheer willpower required to keep a family alive... it's hard to read, but impossible to turn away from. And yet, through all that, there's this persistent thread of hope. Not the cheesy kind, but the hard-won kind, the kind that says: we've been through hell, and still—we write, we love, we keep going.

Heidi has written something so brave here. So human. It reminded me that healing isn't about resolution—it's about looking squarely at what's been hidden for too long, and choosing, again and again, to reach toward the light.

—MELINDA MAYNE